T0059673

Tabitha's Travels

by Arnold Ytreeide

Jotham's Journey: A Family Story for Advent

Bartholomew's Passage: A Family Story for Advent

Tabitha's Travels: A Family Story for Advent

Ishtar's Odyssey: A Family Story for Advent

Amon's Adventure: A Family Story for Easter

Amon's Secret: A Family Story of the First Christians

Tabitha's Travels

A Family Story for Advent

Arnold Ytreeide

KREGEL
PUBLICATIONS

Tabitha's Travels: A Family Story for Advent

© 2003, 2010 by Arnold Ytreeide
All rights reserved.

Second edition published in 2010 by Kregel Publications, a division of Kregel Inc., 2450 Oak Industrial Dr. NE, Grand Rapids, MI 49505.

Cover design and illustrations: Hile Illustration and Design, Ann Arbor, MI.

All rights reserved. No part of this book may be reproduced, stored in a retrieval system, or transmitted in any form or by any means—electronic, mechanical, photocopy, recording, or otherwise—without written permission of the publisher, except for brief quotations in printed reviews.

Scripture taken from the HOLY BIBLE, NEW INTERNATIONAL VERSION®. NIV®. Copyright © 1973, 1978, 1984 by International Bible Society. Used by permission of Zondervan. All rights reserved.

Within the story narrative, Scripture quotations are from the Kings James Version or the New International Version.

Other than biblical characters and events, the persons and events portrayed in this work are the creations of the author, and any resemblance to persons living or dead is purely coincidental.

Library of Congress Cataloging-in-Publication Data
Ytreeide, Arnold
Tabitha's travels : a family story for Advent / Arnold Ytreeide.
   p. cm.
Originally published: Ann Arbor, Mich.: Vine Books, © 2003.
1. Advent—Meditations—Juvenile literature. 2. Christian children—Prayers and devotions. I. Title.
BV40.Y876   2010   242'.332—dc22   2010016281

ISBN 978-0-8254-4172-1

Printed in the United States of America

10 / 25 24 23

For Mom and Dad,
who always supported my
eccentric hobbies and strange
pastimes—such as writing!

A Story for Advent

Stir us up, O Lord, to make ready for your only begotten Son. May we be able to serve you with purity of soul through the coming of him who lives and reigns.

Advent Prayer

Advent. *Adventus. Ecce advenit Dominator Dominus.* Behold, the Lord, the Ruler, is come.

Reaching back two millennia to the birth of the Christ child, and forward to his reign on earth, the tradition of Advent is a threefold celebration of the birth of Jesus, his eventual second coming to earth, and his continued presence in our lives here and now. God in our past, God in our future, God in our present.

Advent.

It started with people going hungry to purify themselves and prepare themselves for holy living. A *fast*, we call it, and such a fast was ordered by the Council of Saragossa in A.D. 381. For three weeks before Epiphany (a feast in January celebrating the divine revelation of Jesus to the gentile Magi), the people were to prepare themselves by fasting and praying. The tradition spread to France in 581 by decree of the Council of Macon, and to Rome and beyond thereafter. Gregory the First refined the season to its present form in about 600 when he declared that it should start the fourth Sunday before Christmas.

Fasting is no longer a part of Advent in most homes and churches (though it wouldn't be a bad idea). For us, Advent means taking time each day, for the three or four weeks before Christmas, to center our thoughts on Truth Incarnate lying in a feeding trough in Bethlehem. It's a time of worship, a time of reflection, a time of focus, and a time of family communion. In the midst of December's commotion and stress, Advent is a few moments to stop, catch your breath, and renew your strength from the only One who can provide true strength.

Tabitha's Travels is one tool you can use to implement a time of Advent in your family—whether yours is a traditional family structure, or one of the many combinations of fathers and mothers, stepparents and grandparents, and guardians and children that make up today's families. You can use this story during Advent even if your family is just you.

Set aside a few minutes each day, beginning the fourth Sunday before Christmas (see the chart on page 159) to light the Advent candles, read the *Tabitha* story and devotional for that day, and pray together. You can also use an Advent calendar (see "Advent Customs," page 9), sing a favorite Christ-centered carol (Frosty's a nice guy but has no place in Advent), and have a time of family sharing.

In our family we set aside fifteen minutes each night before the youngest child goes to bed. Our Advent wreath has a traditional place on a table next to the living room reading chair. The children take turns lighting the candles and reading all the open windows of the Advent calendar, and then adding that day's reading at the end. By the light of the Advent candles I read the last few lines of the previous day's Tabitha story, and then go on to today's story and devotion.

Afterward my wife leads in prayer as we all hold hands. We close by singing one verse of a carol. Then the youngest child lights her own "bedside" candle from the Advent candles and makes her way to bed by candlelight. (This is only for children who are old enough to know how to use a candle safely.) Even when work or visiting takes us out of town, we carry *Tabitha's Travels* and a candle with us and keep our Advent tradition. Sometimes we even get to share our tradition with those we are visiting.

Simple, short, spiritual. A wonderful way to keep the shopping, traffic, rehearsals, concerts, parties, and all the other preparations of December in balance with the reality of God in our lives—past, present, and future.

Advent. *Adventus. Ecce advenit Dominator Dominus.* Behold, the Lord, the Ruler, is come. May God richly bless you and your family as you prepare to celebrate the birth of Christ!

Advent Customs

Advent itself is simply a time set apart for spiritual preparation. But most people associate the word *Advent* with various traditions and customs that have grown up around Christmas in many of the world's cultures. Early in history these customs took the forms of fasts and feasts. Today, they most often take the forms of candles, wreaths, and calendars.

Most churches and families use Advent candles to celebrate the season. Five are used in all, one for each week of Advent and a fifth for Christmas Day. The first, second, and fourth candles are violet, symbolizing penitence. The third is pink, symbolizing joy, and the Christmas Day candle is white, symbolizing the purity of Christ.

Advent candles are usually part of an Advent wreath. While some traditions hang the wreath, it is most commonly used flat, on a table. The circle of the wreath represents the hope of eternal life we have through Christ. The circle itself is made of evergreen branches, symbolizing the abundant life Jesus promised us here and now. The first four candles are positioned along the outside ring of the wreath, and the fifth is placed in the center.

Some traditions use a slanted board instead of a wreath to hold the candles. The board is about four inches by twelve, and raised six inches on one end. Four holes are drilled along the length of the board for the first four candles, and the fifth candle is placed at the top.

Another candle tradition uses one candle for each day of Advent. Any color of candle can be used, but the Sunday candles are usually of a special design and color. The candles can be placed either along a mantel or in holes drilled in a log. Each night during devotions one more candle is lit. By Christmas Day, the candles give bright testimony to and reminder of the evenings of devotion you've spent together as a family.

Advent calendars are popular with children and teach them the Christmas story in an active way. Also called an "Advent house," the calendar is shaped like a house, with a window for each day of Advent. Behind each window is a small portion of the Christmas story (usually from the book of Luke). Each night the family reads the story from these windows, ending with the window for that day.

A Note to Parents: Jesus was not born in an amusement park or religious retreat. He was born into a world of sin, darkness, and death. Indeed, his own birth caused the death of hundreds of male children as Herod sought to kill the new King. So it is not the intent of *Tabitha's Travels* to present a heavenlike world where everyone lives in purity and harmony. While the story is fun and adventurous and has the most happy of endings, it does take place in the real world: there is greed, there is cruelty, there is death. The point is not to cover up the dark side of life but rather to show how the love of God and his Son Jesus Christ is the *light* of our lives.

Most children over the age of seven have been exposed to far worse violence in movies, TV, and cartoons than you'll find in this story. However, if your children are younger than seven, or are particularly sensitive, I suggest you preview each day's reading so that you might skip or summarize the few more tragic parts. You may also want to talk with your children about the events in the story, to help them understand that sometimes bad things happen to people, but that you and God are there to love them and protect them. That is, after all, the reason God sent his Son to us in the first place!

In any event, it is my sincere hope and prayer that you and God together can use this story to teach your children just how much God loves them and how close he is to us, even in times of tragedy.

Especially in times of tragedy.

May God richly bless your Advent time together!

For maps, drawings, a reading quiz, and other special features pertaining to our story, visit www.jothamsjourney.com.

Crossroads

Light the first violet candle.

Elisha, come on!" Tabitha pleaded. "We have to move!" She tugged at the reins with all her might, but the donkey just sat in the middle of the road looking at Tabitha with innocent eyes while the rest of the caravan lumbered by. "Don't look at me like you don't know what I'm saying," Tabitha scolded, the leather reins cutting deep grooves in the palms of her hands. "You know exactly what you're doing!" Tabitha gave one last mighty yank on the reins just as the donkey decided to obey. The donkey stood, the reins went slack, and with all her weight pulling against something that was suddenly no longer there, Tabitha fell backward, sitting down hard in the dust of the trail. A loud laugh slapped at her ears from behind.

"Such fine entertainment you provide, Tabitha," the man laughed from atop his horse. "It will provide a good story for the campfire tonight!" The tall, thin man had a dark beard, and such a long neck that Tabitha thought he looked like a giraffe she had once seen.

"Uncle Hasbah," Tabitha whined, "this dumb donkey won't move!"

"That's why he's called a donkey!" Hasbah replied. Then, more seriously, he added, "Perhaps he simply misses the weight of your grandmother on his back."

"Perhaps," Tabitha said, fondly remembering her grandmother riding this very same donkey.

"Here, hold my horse," Hasbah said, dismounting, "and I'll show you how to get a stubborn donkey to obey." Tabitha did as she was told, taking the reins of the horse as the line of camels, sheep, and shepherds continued to pass by. That her brothers got to be those shepherds while she herself had to cook, clean, and take care of donkeys always frustrated Tabitha. *I can do as much as any boy*, she thought.

"Now, you must take the reins just so," Tabitha's uncle said, wrapping the leather around his hand, "and then give quick little pulls that tell the donkey you are his master." Hasbah did this, but the donkey refused to move.

Irritated, Hasbah pulled harder, but the donkey dug in his feet such that no man in the world could have budged him. But Hasbah was determined to try, and bent low at the waist, leaning back with all his weight. Just then a goat from the passing caravan trotted over and bit Hasbah on the rear end. Hasbah jumped up howling, spun around, and started kicking at the goat. Seeing a reason to move at last, the *donkey* trotted up and bit Hasbah on the rear end.

Tabitha was laughing so hard, she had to hold her sides, but Hasbah just began sputtering angry words as he tried to kick both the donkey *and* the goat. Just then, another man on horseback rode up.

"Brother, what are you doing?" the second man yelled. "Why are you being so cruel to these poor animals?"

"Me! Being cruel! Why I . . . I . . ."

"Stop joking around now," his brother admonished, "and get those animals moving. We must make the Jerusalem road by sundown!"

Hasbah was still fuming and sputtering as Tabitha walked back over to him. Handing him the reins of the horse, she said, "Thank you for a fine lesson, Uncle Hasbah. You surely showed me how to get a donkey moving!"

Hasbah stopped, then finally began laughing at himself. "You are most welcome, my brother's daughter," he said with a bow. "Please call on me any time you need a lesson." With that, he mounted his horse and galloped off toward the head of the line.

With a sigh, Tabitha yanked at the reins of the donkey, and this time he started walking, followed by the goat. As she watched her uncle riding off ahead of her, Tabitha thanked Jehovah once again for her wonderful family.

Tabitha liked the life of the shepherds. Even though she wasn't allowed to watch a flock herself, she liked traveling from this place to that, seeing new sights and meeting new people. Of course, it was usually her brothers who got to have the really fun adventures—fighting off wild animals and thieves, going inside the walls of the biggest cities, and best of all, entering the temple in Jerusalem. *As a girl, I don't get to do any of that*, she thought again with a sigh. But still, being part of a shepherd family was a happy life.

The sun was beginning to slide out of the sky as the caravan snaked over the top of a round, grassy hill. Before them, Tabitha saw a valley rich in grasses, and on the other side, a road running from left to right. Tabitha sucked in her breath at the sight of the road—roads often meant danger from thieves, or worse, Romans. She much preferred it when their family stayed out in the country, far from any roads. Except, of course, when they got to camp at a city.

Far ahead, at the front of the line that was just reaching the floor of the valley, Tabitha saw her father waving his arm over his head in a circle. At once the stream of animals and people began curving to the left, forming itself into a giant oval as it had a thousand times before. *Time to make camp*, Tabitha thought. But she wished her father had chosen some other place, not next to a road.

As the caravan continued to inch forward, and Tabitha got closer to the road, she saw that it ran far off into the distance to the right, but to the left it ran into a steep canyon of angry rocks. Tabitha gulped, thinking what a good place that would be for thieves to hide.

But then Tabitha remembered all the good times she'd had climbing such rocks. When they were younger, her brothers would have make-believe adventures in such places. They'd play Robbers and Romans, fighting each other using sticks for swords. There were only three brothers, though, so the sides were always uneven. Then one day Tabitha had climbed into the rocks to find them. She had picked up a stick and sided with her brother playing the Roman. At first the boys stopped in mid-fight and stared; girls just don't do such things, after all. But then her oldest brother said, "Why not?" and so Tabitha was allowed to play. From then on she was a part of every game, whenever her chores didn't get in the way at least.

When she first saw Tabitha playing with the boys, Tabitha's mother shrieked like a mad camel. Sputtering and scolding, she dragged Tabitha back to the cook tent and put her to work. But then she talked with her husband Eliakim, and together they decided that, really, there's nothing wrong with a girl playing with her brothers, so Tabitha was allowed to have adventures with them once again. As long as they stayed far out from camp, where the other women couldn't see!

Of course, that was only the first of many times that Tabitha would bend people's ideas about what a girl should and shouldn't do. One time her brothers were running from a lioness protecting her cubs. They ran right past Tabitha, who calmly picked up a rock and threw it at the cat as if it were just another tree stump. The cat ran away and the boys were saved, but the only thing the women of the camp could talk about was how improper it was for Tabitha to be throwing rocks!

Another time Tabitha was sewing a new tunic and got the idea that, if you sewed two pieces of leather together just right, they would fit around a man's hands and keep them from getting cut when working with ropes. Thus Tabitha's father was the first man in all of Palestine to have hand coverings. But the women of the camp just complained that girls shouldn't be inventing ways of making work easier.

And then there was the time just the week before when a sheep had fallen into a deep and narrow crevasse. Tabitha's three uncles all stood around shaking their heads and scratching their beards, trying to figure out how to rescue the animal. Tabitha had an idea, but the men kept shooshing her to be quiet. Finally Tabitha left the three men, got a length of rope, and tied it around her waist. Returning to the crevasse where the three uncles were still arguing, she handed the other end of the rope to her uncle Hasbah and climbed down into the crevasse. It wasn't until she jerked on the rope that the red-faced, angry uncles finally noticed what she was doing. They pulled her up easily, and in her arms she carried the wayward sheep. Their faces turning from angry-red to embarrassed-red, the uncles mumbled their thanks, and walked away complaining about a girl not knowing her place!

Finally the mass of people and animals came to a stop, having wrapped itself around the hillsides of the valley. Tabitha saw her brothers each taking their flocks off in different directions, searching for grassy hollows in which to bed their sheep for the night. As for Tabitha and the other women, they knew their jobs without even discussing it. While the men set up the many tents that would house the dozens of aunts, uncles, cousins, and hired workers, the women would start setting up the cook tent and preparing the evening meal. Almost before Tabitha or her donkey had come to a stop, one of the women had a fire started with some dried brush.

Once more, we start our old game, Tabitha sighed to herself. Then, hitching the donkey to a bush, she started unloading its burden of flour, oils, spices, and dried meat. Her thoughts turned to the days ahead, when they'd be visiting a great city and meeting many travelers from distant lands. She thought about the sellers and their goods, about the games she would play with other children, and about the deals her father would make.

It was somewhere in all that thinking, when her chores had become so routine that she didn't even realize she was doing them, and the warmth of the afternoon sun was starting to make her eyelids heavy and her brain begin dreaming of sleep . . . it was just then, as she finished unloading one side of the donkey's pack such that he was leaning out of balance, and the flies had decided that the donkey's head would be a good resting place . . . it was just then, that Tabitha heard the first of the screams.

Tabitha is not what people expect her to be! Her mother, her father, her aunts and uncles—everyone has an idea of how she should behave, what she should be like, what her future will be. So they're surprised, and sometimes upset, when their ideas about Tabitha don't match the reality of Tabitha!

It was just the same with Jesus.

Even though God had told Israel exactly how he was planning to send their Messiah, when Jesus finally arrived, he was not what people expected! Priests, fishermen, carpenters, and midwives—everyone had an idea of how the Messiah should arrive, what he should do when he got here, and how he should shape their futures. So they were surprised, and often upset, when their ideas about Jesus didn't match the reality of Jesus!

Advent is a time for us to focus on the real Jesus of Scripture; a time to get rid of our own ideas about who he is and what he should do for us. It's a time to learn from him how to be servants, to be humble, to love.

We may not fully understand what Jesus is all about, but take these next few weeks to think and learn about the true Christ of Christmas. It's what Advent is all about!

Lost Lambs

Light the first violet candle.

Help!" Tabitha heard the scream again and sucked in her breath. The cry was faint but full of fear.

"Jehovah save me!" the voice echoed. As if lightning had struck the camp, everyone looked up in shock, staring toward the road. "Save me!" the high-pitched voice screeched, and this time it was clear that it came from the canyon.

At once Eliakim dropped the hammer he was using to stake down a tent and sprang to his feet. Tabitha watched from the other side of the valley as her father clambered up the short hill to the road. Before she even could think it, her own feet were running across the meadow, dodging tents and fires and camels. Others were running toward the road as well, Tabitha saw. Other *men*, she noted with disgust. The women mostly cowered behind the tents, or held their children in check.

As for Tabitha, she knew a genuine cry for help when she heard one, and would not hesitate to go to someone in need.

But then she skidded to a stop and stared as her father emerged from the canyon. In his arms he carried a small boy dressed in the tunic of a shepherd. And she saw blood, dripping from the back of the boy's head.

Gulping down her shock, Tabitha forced her feet to move again. By the time she reached her father's side, he had lain the boy gently on the grass, the shadow of his head shading the boy's face. Tabitha held her breath, wondering if the boy was dead. He looked to be about her own age of ten, and seemed to have the face of an angel. *But a dirty angel*, Tabitha thought. His clothes were covered in the dust of the road, and his face smeared with sweat and mud. Without a word, Tabitha reached into her goatskin bag and pulled out a pad of cloth. Handing it to her father, he placed it under the boy's head to stop the bleeding. "I called out to him and he fell," her father explained. "He hit his head on a rock." A moment later, the boy moaned and his eyes fluttered open.

The boy seemed startled, and tried to scramble away. Eliakim held him by the shoulders and said, "There, there, little one. Be at peace." The boy calmed and laid his head back down. "I heard you calling the name of Jehovah," Eliakim said gently. "And so I came."

The boy squinted into the face of Tabitha's father. He opened his mouth to speak, batting his eyes against the sun, but no words would come out. Finally, his voice squeaky and raspy at the same time, the boy spoke.

"You're . . . you're an angel of the Lord," he said, and he lifted a wobbly arm and touched Eliakim's cheek.

Eliakim smiled broadly and chuckled. "No, little one, I am no angel." Then he moved to the side to help the boy sit up and blinding sunlight slapped the boy square in the face. He let out a little yelp and put his hand up to shade his eyes.

"The sun," he whispered hoarsely. "The sun made your hair glow like . . ."

"Shh, shh, I understand," Eliakim said. "But you must rest. I will carry you back to our camp." As powerful arms lifted him from the ground again, a mountain of tension seemed to drain from the boy, and he instantly fell asleep against Eliakim's shoulder. "Tabitha!" he whispered to his daughter. "Fetch water, bread, and fruit. Bring it to our tent."

Tabitha nodded, then lifted her tunic to free her feet and ran toward the cook tent. Her mother saw her coming and yelled out in frustration, "Tabitha! You look like a boy running like that!"

Breathing hard and fast, Tabitha skidded to a stop in front of her mother. "I'm . . . I'm sorry, Mother," she gasped. "But Father has found a small boy who has been injured, and sent me for food and water."

"A boy!" Tabitha's mother exclaimed even as she turned to fill her husband's request. "How did he come to be in such a place? Was he alone?"

Tabitha took the bread and pomegranate her mother held out, then grabbed a skin of water hanging from the tent frame. "I do not know," she answered as she turned away. "But we have seen no one else on the road." With that, Tabitha was off on a dead run again, the food and water huddled in her arms. From behind she heard her mother scolding again. "Tabitha! Don't run! The boy will live while you keep a proper . . ."

But then the voice was gone, lost among the sounds of the caravan animals. Tabitha knew what her mother was saying, though, since she'd heard it many times before. She knew that girls were supposed to remain quiet and dignified, but what use was it to have good running legs if you never let them run?

A crowd had gathered around Eliakim and the boy now, who was lying on a mat in front of the main tent. Tabitha's father took the skin of water from her and poured a few drops in the boy's mouth. The boy didn't stir. Then Tabitha knelt down and held the warm bread under his nose. Her father took the bread and waved it back and forth so that every breath the boy took would be filled with the bread's aroma. A moment later the boy's eyes fluttered open.

The boy's eyes grew wide as he spied the bread, then without warning he snapped at it like a hungry dog jumping at a piece of meat. His mouth took such a big bite of the bread that he also got one of Eliakim's fingers, nipping the end of it.

"Ow!" Eliakim cried. "Careful, little one," he said, shaking his hand quickly to stop the pain. "I know you are hungry, but we have better things to eat than my finger!"

Still without a word, the boy chomped down the piece of bread, and then another held out by Tabitha. When Tabitha held out the pomegranate, she thought the boy's eyes would pop right out of his head. He grabbed the fruit and dove straight into it, its juices dribbling across his chin and down his neck.

Finally, the boy began to slow down and chew the last few bites of the fruit. He looked up for the first time, turning his head this way and that to see all the people around him. "Shepherds," he said after a moment. "You're shepherds."

Eliakim smiled and said, "That is true. As so, too, are you, if I be any judge."

"Yes, sir," the boy answered politely. "I am Jotham of Jericho, defender of the lambs of my father!"

"And I," Tabitha's father said, "am Eliakim, son of Abijah. And who is your father, Jotham of Jericho?"

"He is Asa, son of Jacob," the boy said, drawing his shoulders up square and straight.

Eliakim frowned and stroked his beard. "Hmm, Asa, son of Jacob. I believe I know that name." He thought for a moment, then shook his head. "Ah, well, if I have heard that name I have long forgotten where. But now tell me, why is Jotham of Jericho out on the highway all alone? Where is your caravan?"

The boy's face seemed to get even dirtier as he dropped his gaze to the ground and wrinkled up his forehead. "Well . . . you see . . . I was out in the wilderness watching my sheep. Far from my father's camp. And . . . and a lion came! Yes! A lion! And it killed one of my sheep! And then . . . then . . . then I chased it! I chased the lion across many hills! But finally I caught it! Yes, I did! And . . . and I killed it! With my sling! I hit it with a rock right between its eyes and it dropped dead!"

Jotham paused for a moment, and Tabitha thought it looked like he was trying to decide what happened next. Just as she had so many times before, she felt her heart melt at the thought of someone in trouble. But also as she had many times before, she felt another feeling: the feeling that the boy was lying.

"By the time I got back to my flock," the boy finished his story, "my parents had already been there and left. They . . . they must have thought that the lamb's blood was mine, and thought I was dead. They built a small burial marker with rocks and put my name on top. Anyhow," Jotham said with a sigh, "they left without me, and now I am alone and must find them."

Eliakim stroked his beard for a moment, then said, "So, the great hunter kills a lion with his bare hands, then finds fear in the rocks of a canyon?"

Tabitha saw the boy gulp hard, and knew that her father had the same suspicions as she.

"Uh, well, I was very hungry, and everything looked so strange . . . and I . . . I . . ."

Eliakim smiled again and patted the boy's shoulder. "And you called on the name of Jehovah, which is when I came running to help and startled you."

Jotham lowered his head and nodded. Tabitha could feel the shame inside him, and knew he felt guilty for the lie he had told. "And now," Eliakim said, looking around, "you have new friends to help you find your family and, if you need it, you now have a new family!"

Jotham raised his head again, a smile stretching from ear to ear. Then everyone introduced themselves, and Tabitha waited her turn. First was Uncle Hasbah, then Uncle Ananias, and several aunts, and her older brothers—the list seemed endless. But as she waited patiently, Tabitha heard something shocking.

"Eliakim!" she heard her Uncle Ananias hiss toward her father. This was the uncle Tabitha didn't like much, the one who seemed to only be concerned with himself.

"I must speak with you, brother!" Ananias hissed again.

Tabitha watched as Eliakim turned his attention to his youngest brother. "What is it?" she heard him say.

Moving his mouth close to his older brother's ear, Tabitha's uncle whispered, "The boy is evil! We must get rid of him at once!"

Our God is a God of surprises!

Just when you think everything is going normally, God steps in and says it's time to shake things up a bit: a new job, a new school, new responsibilities. Maybe it's his way of letting us know *he's* in control!

Or maybe he just wants to see if we really trust him.

Either way, our response must be immediate and obedient. "Yes, Lord," is the way we must answer. "Whatever you say. You are in charge!"

Tabitha was just settling in for another normal day when that day was suddenly interrupted. Mary was also having an ordinary day, when suddenly her whole life changed:

> In the sixth month, God sent the angel Gabriel to Nazareth, a town in Galilee,
> to a virgin pledged to be married to a man named Joseph, a descendant of
> David.   LUKE 1:26–27

If you're just expecting a "routine" Christmas this year, maybe you're missing the point. Maybe you're missing the fact that any time we celebrate Jesus, miracles happen!

Brothers

Light the first violet candle.

I have seen it, brother," Ananias continued, rubbing his temples and looking as though he were in a trance. "The boy is trouble. We must send him away!"

Eliakim let out a snort and shook his head in disgust. "If I changed the course of this caravan every time you 'see' something, we'd be going around in circles. The boy stays with us!"

Knowing his older brother's word was final, Ananias didn't argue. But as he walked away in anger he said over his shoulder, "Mark my words, brother! The boy shall be the downfall of us all!"

Tabitha looked back and forth between her retreating uncle and her father. "You will not send Jotham away, will you?" she asked her father.

The long, black beard on Eliakim's chin bounced as he laughed. "No, my daughter, we shall not send the boy away."

As if to seal the statement, Eliakim turned his attention back to Jotham. The others had just finished introducing themselves to the boy. "Master Eliakim," Jotham said, his eyebrows creased into a frown, "have you seen any other caravans since yesterday?"

Eliakim shook his head slowly. "Sadly, no, my friend. We have just come from the hills to the south, and had only just approached this road when we heard your yell."

Jotham's lip began to tremble. "I . . . I was just hoping . . ."

"Yes, I understand. But you are safe now, and I say again that we will help you to find your family. But even if that fails, you may stay with us as long as you wish."

Jotham grinned a great grin, and Tabitha thought what a wonderful day it was that Jehovah should bring her such a friend. "Tabitha," her father said, "show Jotham the camp, then finish your chores for dinner."

"Yes, Father," Tabitha answered. Taking Jotham by the hand, she led him around the tiny valley, pointing out which tent belonged to whom, and where each uncle's animals were kept. Together they watered the lambs, and Tabitha noticed how easily Jotham worked with the tiny sheep. Next they went out among the bushes of a nearby stream and collected dead branches for the fire that night. Suddenly Jotham let out a yelp of pain and started dancing on one foot.

"What is it, my friend?" Tabitha said, dropping her sticks and rushing over to him.

"A scorpion!" Jotham howled in fright. "I've been stung by a scorpion!"

Jotham plopped down in the dirt, threw off his sandal, and held up his foot, crying in panic. Tabitha was scared too—the sting of a scorpion could kill even a large man—but, as always, she acted quickly and calmly. Watching carefully for the offending creature, she knelt down and looked at Jotham's foot. A tiny spot of blood on the sole marked the spot where the stinger had penetrated. But it was a very small sting, Tabitha noted, and didn't have the redness or swelling of other scorpion stings she'd seen. In fact, it didn't really look . . .

Quickly, Tabitha found the sandal Jotham had thrown off. There, in the bottom, with just the very point sticking through the other side, was the thorn of a nearby bush. "That was no scorpion that bit you," Tabitha laughed, "it was a zizyphus bush!"

Jotham stopped wailing and looked at her. "It . . . it was what?" he sniffled.

"A *thorn!*" she said. "You stepped on a thorn."

Jotham's face turned red even as the last of his sobs bounced around inside his chest. "Well . . . ," he said defensively, "it *could* have been a scorpion!"

Tabitha forced her laughter to stay in her belly, realizing she had embarrassed her friend. With just a slight smile on her face she said, "Of course it could have been! It might have even been a snake! But Jehovah has shown us good fortune in making it simply a thorn. Come, let us clean your wound."

Pulling Jotham's arm around her neck, Tabitha helped him hobble over to the stream where she bathed his foot in cool water. After she dried his foot with the bottom of her tunic, she pulled the thorn from Jotham's sandal and tied it back on his foot. Jotham walked hesitantly at first, but by the time they had finished gathering wood and returned to camp, Tabitha noticed he was walking as if nothing had happened. Not wanting to embarrass her friend, she kept the secret of Jotham's panic hidden deep in her heart. Especially when they met her brothers.

The three older boys were returning from the fields just as Tabitha's mother was calling that dinner was ready. Her oldest brother, almost a man, was kind to Jotham, and her youngest brother, barely older than her new friend, was too busy with a cousin to pay much attention. But her middle brother, as she expected, was cruel to the new boy, mocking his story about killing a lion, and laughing at him for his fears. If not for the protection of Tabitha's oldest brother, the boy might have picked a fight with Jotham right then and there.

"Don't let him bother you," Tabitha said to Jotham as she pulled him away. "He's always getting in trouble for being cruel." She was proven right a moment later when Eliakim took his middle son by the ear and led him, squealing, off behind a tent.

Tabitha's entire clan gathered around the cook tent. Eliakim returned, followed by a whimpering middle son, and thanked Jehovah for the meal. Then the men began dishing up their food, followed by the older boys, and then the women. Finally the children were allowed to fill their own bowls. This was the custom, Tabitha knew, and was meant for the survival of the family: if the men were not strong and healthy, then there would be neither food nor safety for any of them.

Tabitha and Jotham sat under an olive tree to eat. As they slurped up their stew, Tabitha's middle brother came over to them. "I am sorry for making fun of you," he said to Jotham, and Tabitha thought that for once he seemed sincere. "Please forgive my rudeness, and accept my friendship in return."

Jotham seemed to study the boy's face for a long moment, and Tabitha thought he had good reason not to trust the boy. But then Jotham smiled and said, "All is forgiven. Come, sit with us and eat."

The brother's face looked a bit tortured. He hesitated a moment, then said, "Well, I believe I shall just stand."

After dinner, as the sun was slipping behind the jagged hills, the entire camp gathered around a fire to relax and tell stories. Several told of small events that occurred during the day, but then people started running out of stories. That's when Tabitha spoke up. "Uncle Hasbah has a story," she said, taunting her favorite uncle.

"I have no such thing!" Hasbah gruffed.

"Surely you do!" Tabitha laughed. "A story of you and Grandmother's donkey!"

"Keep quiet, child," Hasbah threatened in fun, "or I shall fill your bed with goat cheese!"

"I would gladly sleep with the cheese of goats if you will but tell your story!" Tabitha giggled.

"Oh, very well," Hasbah huffed. But just as he opened his mouth to start the story, his brother Uzziah cut in.

"It happened on the trail this afternoon," Uzziah started, and Hasbah looked at him in surprise. Uzziah told the story of how Hasbah had tried to get Tabitha's donkey moving. ". . . So there's Hasbah, pulling at the mule with all his strength, when the goat comes up and bites him on the rear end!" The people erupted in laughter, imagining the sight. "So Hasbah jumps in the air screaming like a buzzard," Uzziah continued. "He spins around and starts kicking at the goat. Then the *donkey* bites him on the rear end!" At this everyone almost fell over, they were laughing so hard, and Hasbah finally spoke up. "And what does my brother do?" he said indignantly. "He rebukes me for being cruel to the animals!"

At this final twist in the story, Tabitha's clan lost all control, laughing hysterically at the folly of the two elders. Finally, as the laughter began to die down, Eliakim stood and moved to the head of the circle. As he did so, Hasbah and Uzziah stepped aside to make room. The others forced the last of their giggles back into their bellies, and waited silently for Eliakim to speak.

"It is written," Eliakim started without introduction, "that Jehovah shall send his Anointed One to bind up the brokenhearted, to comfort all who mourn, and provide for those who grieve. And so we wait. We wait for that Anointed One to appear; we wait for the Messiah to reveal himself to us. But this day," he continued, looking now toward Jotham, "this day Jehovah has brought us one who cannot wait. He has brought one whose heart is broken, one who mourns, and one who grieves. And so," Eliakim said, looking now at the other faces in the camp, the light of the fire dancing on his own, "we ourselves must be like the Messiah to this young one. Even as we wait for Jehovah's Anointed One, we must act as *he* would. We must do what we must to bind the broken heart, comfort him who mourns, provide for him who grieves. It is thus so, and it shall be, in the name of Jehovah."

As one, all those gathered around the fire said, "Selah," and Tabitha wondered if her uncle Ananias would heed his brother's words, or if he would try to harm her new friend, Jotham. She was still wondering late that night as she lay in bed, listening to the crickets, when she heard footsteps creeping up slowly outside the tent.

Jesus has a big job.

At any given time, at least half of the billions of people in this world are in need of help. Some are brokenhearted, some are mourning a loss, some just don't know what to do.

Certainly Jesus can, and does, touch all who are in need. But God also has another plan: he has assigned *us* the honor of being Jesus to those we know and meet. You see, even though Jesus came to earth to save us from our own sins, he also came to show us how to love others. He came to give us our assignment:

> "The Spirit of the Sovereign LORD is on me, because the LORD has anointed me to preach good news to the poor. He has sent me to bind up the broken-hearted, to proclaim freedom for the captives and release from darkness for the prisoners . . . to comfort all who mourn, and provide for those who grieve." ISAIAH 61:1–3

Tabitha's father is wise in knowing that God wants each of us to care for those around us. Wouldn't this Advent season be a good time to practice that more and more?

Suspicions

Light the first violet candle.

The footsteps were quiet like a ghost, and Tabitha had to strain to hear them. But they were there, sneaking up on the tent from the hill behind. Tabitha's parents and brothers were sound asleep, and Jotham lay on his own mat just outside the . . .

Jotham! Instantly Tabitha knew who the night visitor outside the tent was. Whipping back her blanket, she leaped across the forms of her sleeping family like a gazelle, landing lightly between each. On the other side of the tent now, she pulled back the door and slipped out into the night, just in time to see a dark figure bending over Jotham.

"Uncle Ananias!" Tabitha hissed. "What are you doing?!"

Ananias jumped back and let out a little yelp. "Child!" he cried in a whisper. "Don't scare a man so! You'll stop my heart and send me to Jehovah's side!"

"What are you doing to him?" she hissed again, pointing to the sleeping Jotham who lay between them.

"I'm doing nothing to the boy!" Ananias said, indignant. "I only came to see that he remains in his bed, where he can do no mischief."

Tabitha wanted to say that any mischief being done had nothing to do with Jotham, but she knew that she must show respect to her elder even if she didn't trust him. "What are you going to do?" she asked, seeing a bedroll and a cloth under her uncle's arm.

"I'm going to tie one end of this cloth to his ankle," he said, holding up the cloth, "and the other to mine. If he tries to make mischief in the night, I will awaken and stop him!"

"Why do you think him so evil?" Tabitha asked. "He has been nothing but kind and respectful to us."

"He is a wayward orphan and a liar," Ananias spat back. "Such children cannot be trusted!"

That Jotham had lied, Tabitha could not argue. But still . . .

"So you will not harm my friend?" Tabitha asked.

"Of course not!" Ananias answered. "Even if I wanted to, Eliakim has forbidden it, and I know to respect those in authority over me!"

Tabitha nodded at this and said, "Then I will leave you to your connivings and bid you good night."

With that, Tabitha went back inside the tent, amazed that Jotham had slept through the entire exchange. She was still amazed the next morning when he continued sleeping as her entire family stepped over him while leaving the tent. Ananias, she saw, had gone back to his own tent sometime in the night.

Breakfast was served to the men and boys, who then headed out to the fields to graze their flocks. Eliakim announced that they would rest for a day, and that made everyone happy. It was well after the women had eaten their own morning meal, and while Tabitha was helping her mother make a stew, that Tabitha looked up from her work and started giggling like a girl about to be married. In the distance, just coming around a juniper tree, she saw Jotham, with a long, narrow white cloth trailing from his leg. The boy seemed completely unaware that the cloth was stuck to him, or that he was the source of great entertainment for the girl. As he approached, Jotham looked from Tabitha to her mother and back again, the obvious question wrinkled up on his face.

"Good morning, Jotham of Jericho," Tabitha's mother said.

"Good morning, wife of Eliakim."

"Has your long sleep made you well?" she asked.

"Yes, I feel much better today."

Tabitha had sat there giggling through all this, and now her mother scolded her. "Tabitha," she said. "What *are* you going on about?"

Another giggle escaped Tabitha's lips, then she said, "Your forgiveness, Mother. I couldn't help but notice that our new friend has some strange clothes."

Her mother looked to where Tabitha was pointing, then she too began to giggle. Jotham tried not to show any interest, but turned his head slightly and, out of the corner of his eye, checked his clothing.

And then he saw what they were laughing at. "I . . . I . . . ," Jotham stuttered, pulling at the cloth, but Tabitha just laughed.

"Forgive us, Jotham," her mother said, unhooking the cloth and rolling it up. "This is the swaddling cloth in which we wrap newborn babies. It must have been caught in the blanket we gave you." Then, seeing that he was still embarrassed, she added, "Tabitha, why don't you show Jotham your father's camp and tell him of your ancestors?"

"Yes, Mother," Tabitha said with the last of her giggles.

In between viewing tents and talk of family, Tabitha and Jotham spoke of many other things. Tabitha told him of the places they had traveled. "We even visited Jericho once," she said. Jotham beamed at this, proud that she had been to the place of his birth. He told her of the many wonders of Jericho, even though he'd only been there once himself.

"Are you the oldest of your brothers?" Tabitha asked at one point.

"Uh, y-yes," Jotham stuttered. "I am the firstborn of my father!"

"You must be very proud," she said, though in her heart she suspected he was just boasting again.

That afternoon Eliakim called to Jotham to come and speak with him. While he was gone, Tabitha was sent to fetch water from a stream. Jotham joined her there a short while later, stomping down the hill toward the stream, his face red and twisted in anger.

"Jotham! What is it?" Tabitha asked. "What has made you so angry?"

"Your father will not let me search for my family in the direction I know them to be!"

Tabitha thought about this for a long moment. "My father is a very wise man," she said. "And a great one! Once he even saved the life of a Roman in the desert and received a great reward! He must do what is best for you."

"I know this in my head," Jotham answered, "but my heart is saying I must go to the east, toward the sea where nothing lives. I just know I will find my family there!"

"You want to go to the Sea of Death?!"

"No, but I want to find my family. If that is where I must—"

Jotham was interrupted by a man yelling an alarm from across the valley. "Caravan!" he cried. "Caravan approaching!"

Jotham jumped up and ran off toward the line of camels, and Tabitha wondered if she was about to lose her new friend.

Tabitha sees right through Jotham and knows he's lying about his heroism. Jotham is telling those lies so that Eliakim's clan will be impressed.

Most of us, at one time or another, do the same thing. For some reason, we feel like it's not enough that God loves us just the way we are; we decide it's more important for *people* to like us, so we say and do things to make them think we're great.

But the truth is, we don't *need* people to think we're great, because we are all equally important to God. It doesn't matter if you're better at football than someone else, or get better grades, or have more power; in God's eyes, we are all just as good and just as valuable.

"If anyone thinks he is something when he is nothing, he deceives himself," Galatians 6:3 tells us. But Jesus doesn't deceive us. He came to earth to say to each of us, "God loves *you!*"

What better Christmas present could there be?

Good Intentions

Light the first violet candle.

C aravan!" came the cry again.

Tabitha strained to see over the top of the hill. Across the valley, on the road she so feared, rose a billowing cloud of dust from the hooves and feet of the caravan army. They weren't shepherds, she could see. At least no shepherds she'd ever known. And not traders, either. While the leader wore a coat of many colors, the rest of the people were dressed in an odd mix of rags and tunics and Roman garb.

"I wonder who they are," Tabitha said to herself. Jotham returned a few minutes later, running and out of breath.

"I am leaving with this caravan and your father said to give me the donkey that your grandmother rode!"

"You're leaving?" Tabitha asked, the pain of the words wavering in her voice.

"I must!" Jotham answered. "I must find my family!"

As they climbed the hill and unhitched the donkey, Tabitha asked, "Will you come back, Jotham of Jericho?"

"I promise I will! Once I find my father, I will tell him of the kindness Eliakim has shown me. Then we will find you, and my father will meet your father, and we will have a great feast!"

Tabitha's mother brought a bag filled with dried meat and fruits. But Tabitha's heart felt like an empty bag. Inside she cried at the thought of losing her new friend so soon. "I will bake bread every day so it will be fresh when you return," she said as Jotham prepared to leave.

"May Jehovah reward your kindness with a thousand head of sheep," was Jotham's reply. He turned and started to leave, but then stopped and came back. "I . . . I'm not really the firstborn of my father," he said, his head hung low. "I am the youngest."

Tabitha smiled. "I know," she said.

Jotham looked up in surprise, then he, too, smiled. Then he turned and led the donkey to the end of the caravan, and soon the line of animals started moving again, and disappeared over the hill. Tabitha watched until the last of the dust settled, then sighed a deep sigh and turned back to her chores.

Days seemed to drag for Tabitha after that. Her father ordered the caravan to move again, and they continued west, opposite the direction Jotham had gone. Only when the great city of Hebron came into view did Tabitha forget her sadness for a time.

The city was surrounded by a wall that seemed to reach to the clouds. Everywhere she looked, Tabitha saw camps of shepherds, traders, and travelers. Inside the city gates, the sights and smells were even more spectacular. Billowing fabrics that almost hurt Tabitha's eyes, so bright were their colors. Chunks of meat sizzled on thin sticks, and pastries fresh from a baker's oven smelled of honey and almonds. Sellers sold everything a shepherd could want and more: bowls and toys and tents and tunics. It was enough to make Tabitha wonder why anyone bothered to make their own things when they could come to a place such as this and simply buy them.

And then there were the people, packed into the narrow streets from one side to the other, pushing and jostling and forcing their way through. But Tabitha didn't mind; it was just so nice to be with other people!

And animals! Monkeys on leashes, birds in cages, snakes in baskets. It almost seemed as if Noah had landed his ark right here in Hebron and let all the animals out.

Tabitha held tightly to her father's hand as they pressed through the crowd. She had begged to come with him, and was afraid that her older sister Rachel would get to instead. But Rachel was scared and had stayed with their mother. So now Tabitha found herself in her favorite place—doing something that girls weren't supposed to do.

"Where are we going, Father?"

"To find a man named Zadok of Kadesh," Eliakim answered.

Tabitha almost slipped in the mud of the steep street, but her father pulled her up easily, setting her back on her feet. "Will we buy from him more sheep?" she asked.

"No, we are here to sell him some sheep," Eliakim answered. "The best tenth of our flock."

"Why do you want to sell a tenth of our flock?"

"So that we may go to the city of my birth and pay our family taxes."

"What are taxes?" Tabitha asked.

"Money we pay to the Romans for building roads and protecting us."

Such an idea was strange to Tabitha, but she said no more about it. Finally they reached an open courtyard with several large tents set up around the outside. Men stood in small groups talking and laughing and arguing. Several of the men looked suspiciously at Tabitha, and at first she felt she shouldn't be there. But then she saw that many of the men had their sons with them, some much younger than Tabitha. *If they can have boys here*, she thought, *then they can have girls, too!*

Tabitha followed her father as he went from tent to tent, finally finding what he was looking for. He entered a tent of red and orange stripes, with Tabitha right behind him. Inside it was dark for a moment, then Tabitha's eyes decided to see into the darkness and she saw a dozen men sitting on pillows in a circle on the floor. Oil lamps hung from several of the poles holding up the tent, and gave off enough light that soon Tabitha could see clearly. What she saw, she didn't like. Everyone was looking at *her*.

"You bring a girl into the tent of Zadok?" a large man asked.

Eliakim bowed politely. "By your favor," he said, "I bring that which is most precious to me to honor he who is most gracious to all."

The fat man nodded and smiled. "If this is indeed what is most precious to you," he said, "then truly you honor me. Come, sit. We shall talk."

Following her father, and feeling very conspicuous, Tabitha sat in the circle of men. She heard a few clucks and grumbles from the others, but Tabitha didn't care. Her father had called her his most precious possession, and that made all the world right!

It was obvious that Eliakim and Zadok had known each other for years, and they spent much time giving and taking news and stories of those years. Tabitha's head began to nod, and she had to force her eyes to stay open. Sitting cross-legged on the soft pillow, she rocked back and forth as she'd fall asleep for a moment, then jerk herself awake. Finally Zadok looked at her, smiled, and said, "Perhaps we should move on to our business, before your Precious finds her dreams."

Eliakim cleared his throat in embarrassment, but began the negotiations in any event. He offered Zadok the best tenth of his flock, and Zadok offered a price. Eliakim respectfully declined the offer, saying he could get much better at the next tent over. Back and forth they went, until finally they reached a price they could both be happy with. Tabitha watched all this, impressed with how firm, but polite, her father was. The deal was made, the money was paid, and Eliakim told Zadok he could send men to select the sheep.

"Camel breath!" Zadok said with a wave of his hand. "You choose and send them over. If I cannot trust Eliakim, son of Abijah, then there is no more reason to live, let alone trade!"

Eliakim bowed at the compliment, and then a thick, black beverage was served to all the men in celebration of the deal. As they drank, Eliakim told of their latest travels, and eventually told of finding a lost boy. Tabitha saw Zadok look up in surprise, but Eliakim didn't notice and just kept talking. Finally Zadok interrupted.

"This boy, you say he was a shepherd without a family?"

"That is the truth," Eliakim answered.

"And what of his family?"

"They thought him killed by a wild animal. They do not know he is alive."

Zadok stood and paced the floor. It seemed to Tabitha that she could see the thoughts racing inside his head until, finally, he stopped, looked at Eliakim, and said, "The boy's father was here in this tent not two days ago!"

Tabitha's heart raced at the thought that they might find her friend's family. Eliakim seemed unperturbed and simply quizzed Zadok about what he had seen. When he was satisfied, he said, "I believe you are correct in this, master Zadok. Perhaps we should work to reunite this family with their son."

"But you said the boy is on a caravan headed east," Zadok replied.

"So he is," Eliakim said. "But three men on fast camels could easily catch them in a day or two."

Finally one of the other traders spoke up. "This caravan," he said suspiciously, "what was it like?"

Eliakim gave a thorough description. As he did so, Tabitha saw the man's face go pale and his body slumped just a bit. When Eliakim had finished, the trader looked at him in horror. "That was the caravan of Decha of Megiddo," he gasped. "Master Eliakim, you have given the boy Jotham to a murderer!"

Eliakim has made a terrible mistake. He entrusted Jotham to what he thought was a family of traders, but was instead a band of thieves.

Sometimes *we* make mistakes, too. Sometimes large, sometimes small, but often, mistakes that hurt other people.

Should Eliakim now give up because he made such a mistake? Should we? Or should we understand that being imperfect is just a part of being human?

To paraphrase Psalm 19:12, 14, "Who can understand his own mistakes? Lord, forgive my hidden faults! . . . Even so, may the words I speak and the things I think make you happy, Lord, my Rock and my Redeemer."

Even though Jesus was perfect, he lived with a lot of imperfect people. Over and over, instead of condemning people for their mistakes, he forgave them, encouraged them, and told them how to live better lives once they had turned away from the old ones.

Advent is a time when we celebrate a new beginning. Maybe it would be a good time to celebrate something new for you; maybe it would be a good time to forgive yourself for your mistakes.

Servant Girl

Light the first violet candle.

The name "Decha of Megiddo" hung in the air like the stench of burned meat. Tabitha watched her father's face, which was frozen in a look of death. He stared at the trader, so shocked that even his tongue wouldn't move. Finally his chin began to wobble, and he forced a rasping whisper from his mouth.

"Decha . . . ?" he said, and paused. "Decha of Megiddo? That . . . that cannot be! He is far to the north, near the lake of Galilee!"

The other trader shook his head rapidly. "No, no, no," he said, "he was here just these last few days. His entire caravan camped here for a week. Uriah saw him! Tell him, Uriah!" He turned to another trader, who nodded.

"It is true," the second man said. "I saw him with my own eyes!" Several other men murmured their agreement.

Eliakim's knees went weak, and he sank to the pillows. "What have I done?" he moaned. "That poor boy Jotham . . . in the clutches of that thief!"

Tabitha had never seen her father like this. She remembered how he always knew the answer to any question asked, how he gave orders without hesitation, solved problems with barely a thought. He was confident and sure! But what she saw before her now was a man in terrible guilt and terrible pain.

Zadok and the other traders wished Eliakim well, then left the tent so as not to embarrass their friend. Tabitha stayed with her father, though, wondering how to help him. Eliakim just sat, staring straight ahead. *It's as if he had killed Jotham*, Tabitha thought.

And suddenly, she realized.

Tabitha's insides began to shake then, at the thought that Jotham might be dead. "Do you really think this evil man would harm Jotham?" she asked.

Eliakim turned and stared blankly at his daughter. "Decha of Megiddo is the most treacherous of all villains. He would kill his own mother for a piece of stale bread!"

Tabitha had never heard her father speak such angry words in her whole life and couldn't figure out why he did now. But what she did know was that her father was in great pain, and *that* she could do something about.

"I lift up my eyes to the hills," she started softly, "where does my help come from?" They were words she had learned from the poems of the Torah, words she now used to comfort her father. "My help comes from the Lord," she continued, "the Maker of heaven and earth."

A man could have eaten a heavy meal in the time Eliakim sat listening, but finally he closed his eyes, then opened them slowly, and looked at his daughter. "Your words are a powerful cure," he said to Tabitha. And then he smiled, which made Tabitha relax. "I have been considering our course," he continued, "and Jehovah has revealed it to me clearly."

Eliakim stood quickly and went to the entrance of the tent. He called the trader back in. "Zadok, my friend," he said. "Would you trade three horses for four of my camels?"

"You'll have three of my finest," Zadok replied.

"Then I will send for them within the hour." Holding his hand out to Tabitha he said, "Come, we must hurry. There is much to do."

Tabitha felt herself pushed this way and that as her father tore through the crowd. She barely noticed the fire dancers, saw only one juggle from the jugglers, and never did find the source of the lute music. Then they had reached the other side of the city, passed through the Dung Gate in the wall, and were back at their camp before Tabitha had blinked twice, it seemed. As they approached, Eliakim yelled, "Hoy-ay! Hoy-ay!" By the time they stood at the fire circle, the entire clan had gathered to hear the alarm.

"My brothers," Eliakim said to Tabitha's uncles. "I have done a terrible thing. I have released the boy Jotham into the clutches of Decha of Megiddo!" A loud cry swept across the family, some because they realized what was happening to Jotham, some because they realized the thief had ridden right through their camp without their knowing it. "We must go and rescue the boy at once," Eliakim continued. "Hasbah! Uzziah! You and I will leave within the hour! Horses have been arranged. Go now, and pack lightly. Ananias," he said to his youngest brother, "you must lead our flock to the gates of Bethlehem. When we have found the boy, we will meet you there. In your travels, watch for Jotham's family, and tell them he is alive." Eliakim thought about that for a moment, then added, "At least we hope he still is."

With a clap of his hands Eliakim dismissed the group, then went to his tent where his wife and daughters were already gathering his things. As Eliakim hurried about, collecting knives and tools and bedding, Tabitha followed him, pulling at his tunic.

"Father! Father!" she said. "I have a thought!"

"Yes, Tabitha," Eliakim replied as he dug through the contents of a bag. "What is it?"

"Your mission is much too important for you to worry about cooking food or building fires. You must spend all your time in your investigations. You must take a woman with you to care for the camp, to cook your food, to mend your clothing!"

Eliakim shook his head like a dog shaking off water. "No. No. It will be much too dangerous."

"But Father," she insisted, "you need someone to care for your needs while you do the work of a man!"

Eliakim suddenly realized what his daughter was doing. He tried to hide a smile, and teased her a bit as he packed. "Perhaps you are right. Perhaps our task will be done more quickly if we have help. Go tell your brother Saul he is going with us."

"Saul!" Tabitha cried. "He can't go! He must stay to watch his flock!"

"Oh yes, yes, you are correct," Eliakim said. "But what can I do? It must be a son who accompanies me."

"Why a son?" Tabitha said, more angrily than she would normally talk to her father. "A girl is every bit as good as a boy! We can do anything a boy can do, and more!" she lectured. "Can a boy cook a fine stew? Can a boy sew a torn tent? Will a boy wash his father's feet after a long day?"

Eliakim stopped his work to rub his chin and think. "Very well then, I guess it will have to be a daughter." Tabitha grinned a wide grin as her father looked at her, but then Eliakim looked to the other side of the tent and said, "Rachel! Pack your things! You're going with us!"

Rachel looked up in shock from where she was helping her mother. "I . . . I am to go . . . on a *horse*?"

"Yes, now quickly pack."

"But *Father*," the older girl cried, "I don't want to go off chasing thieves and sleeping in the dirt!"

"Father!" Tabitha whispered, pulling at his tunic. "Father!"

"Yes, Tabitha?" Eliakim answered.

"Why would you choose a rose to do the work of a thorn?"

Eliakim nodded slowly. "Perhaps you are right," he whispered back. Then calling across the tent again he said, "Rachel, you may stay with your mother. Tabitha shall accompany me."

Tabitha grinned again, and her father smiled, showing that he knew all along it would come to this. "Quickly now," he said, "pack a few clothes. The sun will not wait for us."

A short while later the sheep and camels had been delivered, the horses had been fetched and loaded, and the rescuers were ready to leave. Prayers were said, and greetings of "Safe travel!" given. "May you find the boy Jotham before his journey leads to peril," Ananias said, and it surprised Tabitha. Then the three men mounted their horses and Eliakim pulled Tabitha up in front of him. With a kick of their heels they had the animals moving, returning down the road their caravan had traveled just two days before.

And as the great city of Hebron disappeared behind them, Tabitha wondered what adventures lay ahead, and if they would find her friend Jotham before any harm came his way.

I no longer call you servants, because a servant does not know his master's business. Instead, I have called you friends, for everything that I learned from my Father I have made known to you.   JOHN 15:15

These words of Jesus tell us one of the reasons he came to earth: to let us know that God wants to be friends with us. Abraham had been called a friend of God many centuries before this, but, until Jesus made it clear, probably few people thought about God as a friend.

So what does it mean to be friends with the Son of God? What do friends do for each other? How do they treat each other?

One answer would be that friends will do anything for each other—even give up their lives. Which is, of course, exactly what Jesus did for us. How can we show him our friendship in return? How would he like to see us behave?

Eliakim is not *required* to attempt a rescue of Jotham. He could just go about his business, and no one would ever know or care that he once knew the boy. But Eliakim is a friend of both Jotham and God, so he must act as Jesus would in the same situation—he must be willing to give up the life he has known to be like Jesus to someone else.

How can you be like Jesus to others in your life?

En Gedi

Light the first violet candle.

*I*f I were a boy, Tabitha thought to herself, *I'd be whining and complaining right now!*

Sitting in front of her father on a horse that had only a blanket for a saddle, Tabitha's backside was getting sore. *By the end of the day*, she continued her thinking, *I'll be sitting on blisters!*

But girls don't complain, she knew. That's for boys to do. Girls must learn to be patient and endure much pain without grumbling, so they can grow into quiet and respectful wives. *That* was a thought Tabitha didn't much like! To not complain about pain or discomfort was fine, but she had no intention of being a wife who did nothing and said even less!

Passing through the canyon where they had first met Jotham, Tabitha felt like their journey was just starting, even though they had already been on the road a day. So far all they had done was return to where they had started. Now they would be on *new* roads, with new perils and adventures waiting.

As the hours dragged on, the heat of the sun and the bones of the horse's spine worked together to make Tabitha miserable. Still, she decided, it was all worth it, because it meant long conversations with her father.

"But Naomi did what God wanted her to," Tabitha said, debating with her father the story from the Torah.

"Yes, she did," her father answered. "But that doesn't mean no harm could come to her. Other people had the freedom to act against God, just as she had freedom to follow him."

Tabitha sighed. "I don't understand why Jehovah doesn't just make everyone follow him. Then the world would be so simple!"

"Yes, it would," her father said. "But it would also make it very ordinary. Everyone would be the same!" As Tabitha thought about this, Eliakim looked at his daughter. "I have never understood why women are not allowed to learn the Torah. You learn it easily and care about it deeply," he said, and Tabitha smiled.

The debate continued, as did the journey. The sun was just beginning to slide out of the sky when Eliakim came to a stop. There was a small meadow to the side of the road, surrounded on three sides by trees. The grass of the meadow had been trampled down, and it was obvious that a large caravan had stopped there recently, probably just the night before.

Eliakim dismounted and surveyed the site. Soon he found two ropes hanging from an olive tree, and he studied them intently. Tabitha and her two uncles came up behind her father.

"Someone was hung up here by the arms," he said finally, noticing a bit of blood on the ends of the rope. "Someone small," he added, then looked at Tabitha. "Someone about your size."

The impact of her father's words struck Tabitha like a fist. "Jotham!" she gasped.

"Perhaps," answered her father. "Though we cannot know if this be true. Still, the height of the ropes is right." Then looking around he added, "And the camp broke in haste. Otherwise they would not have left such fine rope, or that pot over there, or the blanket in that tree." Eliakim mulled all this over. "Yes," he said finally, "something happened here. Something that made Decha leave in a hurry."

It was the first time her father had said that name since leaving Hebron, and the first time it made her skin crawl. *Decha of Megiddo is no longer a ghost in someone else's dreams*, she thought as she looked about the camp. *He is a real man. A real demon.*

"If Decha left in haste, then so must we," Eliakim said. "Even though he has half a day's lead on us, he is traveling with a caravan, and we can overtake them if we can but find the way."

With that, the three men and their young handmaiden mounted the horses and set off down the road at twice the pace they had been traveling. Now Tabitha couldn't help but let out an occasional cry as the horse bounced and swayed, pounding away at the dirt. Tears came to her eyes from the wind in her face. As the sun dropped lower in the sky behind them, long, thin shadows of their galloping horses spread out ahead of them on the road as if to clear the way for very important travelers.

In the very last of the light, just before they would no longer be able to see the road ahead of them, they reached the top of a hill overlooking a lake so large that Tabitha couldn't see the other side.

"The Sea of Death," Tabitha gasped.

"It is so," Eliakim said. "And there, En Gedi."

Tabitha hadn't even noticed at first, but sitting on a plateau below them, but above the water, was a walled city. It glowed with the light of a thousand torches from inside the walls, and now Tabitha could hear lively music of flutes and strings. And screaming.

"Hebron is a temple compared to this place," Eliakim said in disgust. Then to his daughter added, "You must stay close, and never let go of my tunic."

Wide-eyed and trembling a bit, Tabitha nodded her agreement to these rules.

Eliakim kicked his horse into motion and the four travelers headed down the hill. A guard in a window above the city gate stopped them with a shout and asked their business.

"We are here to acquire a small boy," Eliakim answered, not wanting to lie but not wanting to tell the whole truth either.

"Ah, a husband for your daughter there!" the guard shouted, and the thought of it made Tabitha's insides wrinkle up. "A good place to shop, En Gedi!" he added. "But you must leave your horses outside the gate."

Eliakim hesitated, knowing this town was thick with thieves, but he knew they had no choice. Leaving Hasbah to guard their steeds, he entered through the gate, with Tabitha and Uzziah close behind.

En Gedi was about half the size of Hebron, Tabitha decided immediately, but with four times the people! Bumped and thumped and jostled at every step, all Tabitha could see were bodies much taller than herself. Then she discovered that, by looking straight up, she could see the many windows on the upper floors of the buildings on either side of the street, and there she saw women in colorful scarves, men swaying from drunkenness, and everyone singing along with the music that seemed to fill the entire city.

Finally they reached an open courtyard and Eliakim pulled them all over to the side. They found one empty, wooden table among several occupied ones outside an inn. Tucked in between two walls that formed a corner, the inn gave visitors a bit of breathing room. A man came and asked what they wanted, and Eliakim ordered food for all three of them, plus some to take back to Hasbah. Tabitha had never before seen a place where you sit at a table and order food, and her father explained it was something the Greeks had started.

Large bowls of lamb stew appeared before the three travelers, and they ate in silence. Tabitha was fascinated with all the dancing and music and magicians and sellers that passed before them. It was all very exciting, but also frightening, and she ate her entire bowl of stew while tightly grasping the hem of her father's tunic.

"Stay with your uncle now," Eliakim told Tabitha after he finished his meal. "I must see about Jotham."

Tabitha didn't much like her father leaving her, but Uncle Uzziah was strong and tall, and his tunic good for hanging onto.

As they waited for Eliakim to return, Tabitha watched the wonders and the evils of the scene before them. But she noticed that Uzziah was only watching one particular pair of men. They were hiding in a doorway across the street, and looked like greasy weasels. Every time the crowd would part enough to clear the view, there would be the two men, staring at Tabitha and whispering.

"Tabitha!" Uzziah said, handing her his head covering. "Put your hair up and wrap it in this." Tabitha looked shocked, but obeyed in silence. A few minutes later, Tabitha's long hair had disappeared, and was replaced by the head covering of a man . . . or boy.

Suddenly, the weasels were gone. The crowd had parted again, but now the doorway was empty. Uzziah put his hand on the hilt of the knife in his belt and looked around frantically. Holding Tabitha tightly with his other hand, he strained to see into every corner and behind every cart.

A hand clamped on Uzziah's shoulder! Uzziah jumped up and drew his knife in one swift motion. He was just ready to swing his blade when the hand caught his wrist and held it tightly.

"Brother, did I offend you in some way?" Eliakim asked with a smile.

Sheepishly, the shepherd dropped his arm and slid his knife back in his belt.

"Forgive me, brother," he said. "It was two thieves, not you, I suspected of offense."

Eliakim gave a strange look at Tabitha. "Did you trade my daughter for a son?" he asked Uzziah.

"No," Uzziah answered seriously. "The two thieves took too great an interest in Tabitha. I thought it wise to make her less attractive."

"Wise indeed," Eliakim said. "Then let us leave this place," he added, pulling Tabitha to her feet, "and be off on our rescue of Jotham."

"You found news of him?" Tabitha gasped.

"Indeed," Eliakim answered. "Though I'm not sure if the news be good or bad."

As they pushed their way back toward the gate, Eliakim told the others what he had learned. "The same day that Jotham left our camp," he told them, "he was brought here by one of Decha's men. He was trying to sell the boy as a slave, but a fool jumped in and saved him."

Tabitha looked up at her father with huge eyes. "A *fool!*" she said. "What *kind* of fool?"

"A foolish one, I would presume," her father said as he pushed yet another drunken man aside. "Or perhaps not. I also heard a rumor that the fool is really a monk from Qumran who only dresses as a fool to hide his identity."

"What's a Qumran?" Tabitha asked.

"A small compound in the desert where monks work to make copies of the Torah," her father answered. "That is where we are headed now, though you will have to wait outside."

Tabitha looked up in surprise. "Why can't I go inside?" she asked, indignant.

"Only men and boys are allowed inside the walls of Qumran," Eliakim answered. "It is their way."

Tabitha was just about to say that it wasn't *her* way, when they finally reached the city gate. Following her father through, Tabitha was staring at the ground thinking angry thoughts about Qumran when suddenly her father stopped. She looked up and her heart lurched. Standing on the other side of their horses, and surrounding her Uncle Hasbah, was a squad of Roman soldiers.

"You!" the leader of the Romans shouted from atop his horse, pointing his spear at Eliakim. "What is your name and where have you come from?"

Tabitha heard her father swallow hard before he answered. "Eliakim, son of Abijah. We come from Hebron, and before that, the hills of Judea."

The Roman jumped off his horse and stormed over to Eliakim. "Liar!" he roared. "You are a monk who posed as a fool and stole this boy from his master in Caesarea, and you are under arrest!"

Fear is a strong emotion that keeps us from enjoying life. Sure, sometimes there's good reason for our fear; sometimes bad things do happen to people when they don't deserve them. Other times, like with Tabitha at the inn, we're in danger and don't even realize it.

We don't really know what lies around the next corner or within the next year, but there is one thing we can know: Jesus will be right there with us, protecting us, guiding us, or simply helping us endure, no matter what.

> Surely God is my salvation; I will trust and not be afraid. The LORD, the
> LORD, is my strength and my song; he has become my salvation.
>
> ISAIAH 12:2

Give your fears to God—fears about the future, fears about other people, fears about yourself. He'd love to take your fears and give you peace and joy in return. Why not let him?

False Arrest

Light the first two violet candles.

Tabitha felt her knees go weak and thought her legs would not hold her as Roman soldiers circled her and her father. But she was confident this would all be cleared up in a moment. Ripping the covering from her head she shouted at the Roman, "I'm no boy! I'm his daughter, Tabitha!"

The Roman stood back in shock. He stared from Tabitha to her father and back several times. Finally his eyes narrowed and his forehead wrinkled. "What game is this you play?" he asked. "Do you try to make fools of the Roman Legion!"

"No! No!" Eliakim stammered. "Some thieves were watching my daugh—"

"Silence!" the Roman shouted. Then in a low growl he said, "I have searched a month for the runaway slave boy and his fool friend. I must now report back to the procurator in Jerusalem, and I will not go there without a Jew in custody." Looking around for a moment, he suddenly turned to Eliakim and said, "Show me the bill of sale for these three horses!"

Eliakim went pale. "We . . . we traded for them in Hebron and left quickly. There was no time for—"

"Seize them!" the Roman commander roared, and immediately Eliakim and his two brothers closed in. "You are under arrest for thievery!" the centurion yelled.

Tabitha screamed as the soldiers ripped her hand from her father's tunic and pushed him forward. She pulled at the Roman leader's cape, but he turned and kicked her down with his foot, then mounted his horse. "Father!" she cried. "Please don't take my father!"

But the Romans didn't even slow down. Eliakim fought to free himself, to protect his daughter. But three Romans held him tightly, tied his arms behind his back, and tied the rope to one of their horses.

The anger of a mad camel took over Eliakim and he rammed and kicked the three soldiers until they were lying on the ground. Free of his captors for a moment, but with his arms still tied, he shouted at the centurion, "I am a citizen of Rome! You have no right to treat me so!"

Instantly all the soldiers stopped and stared. The centurion leaned over, low in his saddle, to get a closer look.

"You're no Roman," he said after careful inspection. "You are a dog Jew—a shepherd, and a liar!"

"I am a citizen of Rome," Eliakim said defiantly. "And I will see you hung for this cruel treatment unless you release me at once!"

The centurion eyed his prisoner slowly, then said, "If you be a citizen, then you will have the parchment to prove it."

For the first time, Eliakim seemed a bit unsure of himself. "I have such a parchment," he said, and the Roman looked up in surprise. "They are with my family in Hebron."

A look of disgust crossed the centurion's face. "A lie like all the rest!" he said. Then to the soldiers he commanded, "Mount!"

"Tabitha!" Eliakim cried as the soldier jerked him into motion. "Tabitha!" he called again over his shoulder. "Run to Qumran, a day to the north! Find someone to help you to Hebron! Tell Ananias to bring my scrolls to Jerusalem!"

The centurion kicked his horse into action and yelled to his men, "Ride!"

A dozen horses now galloped up the road, dragging Eliakim and his two brothers.

"Father!" Tabitha screamed as she watched the three men stumbling to keep up with the horses. "Please! Please don't take my father!"

Then they were gone into the night.

Alone, Tabitha sat in the dust of the road, crying for her father. She also mourned the fact that she was now alone, abandoned outside one of the most evil cities she had ever . . .

Tabitha suddenly looked up, toward the city gate. The guard in the window above was eyeing her. He whispered something to another man, who left the window quickly. Tabitha gulped down her fear and sorrow and forced herself to her feet. Swinging around this way and that looking at the stars and the moon, she finally found north, as her father had taught her. Behind her, the city gates creaked, and she decided she didn't want to wait and see who was coming out. As fast as her sandaled feet would take her, she ran off into the night, up the road that led to the north.

Tabitha had traveled only a few hundred paces when she heard footsteps in the dirt behind her. She couldn't see anything in the moonlight, but knew someone was there. The roadway was close to the sea at this point, but far above it. How far, Tabitha could not tell. Jumping over the side of the road, she hoped it was a gradual slope. She also hoped there were no snakes out this night. As she slipped over the edge and began to fall, she grabbed at a bush and hung there. Her feet could find nothing but the air below.

As the bush's roots weakened, and Tabitha felt herself slipping down the hill toward the Sea of Death, she heard a voice hissing out of the darkness above. "Small girl!" the voice called. "Come to me now! Come to me *now*," the voice said again, "and I will hurt you less!"

> Though an army besiege me, my heart will not fear; though war break out against me, even then will I be confident. PSALM 27:3

Could you really pray that prayer and mean it? Could you really face an army of problems, a war of personal attacks, and not be afraid?

Why does God allow terrible things to happen to his people? Why doesn't he simply step in and keep evil out of our lives?

That's a very old question that has a very old answer: God has given us the freedom to choose his way or not. We can choose to accept him and treat others with love, or to reject him and be selfish. But he can't give us freedom of choice one minute and take it away the next minute; he can't give freedom of choice to one person and not to someone else.

In short, he has to give evil people the same freedoms he gives all his children.

So bad things continue to happen. What God can and will do, though, is be with us through those times, no matter what. He'll hold our hands, give us strength to endure, and ultimately, see us through to the victory of eternal life with him.

Secrets

Light the first two violet candles.

Tabitha felt her fingers slipping down the slick branches of the bush. At the same time the bush was pulling out of the hillside, so that she didn't know which would be the end of her, only that it would happen very soon. She heard the footsteps of the devil above her on the road, and knew that his searchings would soon lead to her.

"Small girl!" the man hissed again, "I know you are here! Take care you don't step on an asp! They are everywhere here!"

Tabitha shivered at the thought of stepping on a poisonous snake, but knew the man was just trying to get her to make a noise. The bush gave a little jerk as another root pulled free and she dropped a few more inches. The sandal on her left foot was thrown loose and she felt the cool night air on her bare toes.

With one last *snap*, the bush pulled out of the hillside. Tabitha slid down the slope and over the edge. This time she could not hold her screams inside. As she fell out into the open air she let out a loud cry. But it was only a moment before she hit soft earth, and she realized the hill she had been hanging from was only slightly taller than herself. Some other time she might have laughed at her folly, but her cry had caught the attention of the villain, and now she could see his shadow coming toward her in the moonlight.

Tabitha grabbed her sandal and held it up like a sword as she backed away from the man, fear trembling in every bone. He jumped from the road to the point where she had landed moments before. As he flew through the air, his tunic and overcoat billowed in the wind, making him seem larger than life. He landed with a thud, never taking his eyes off Tabitha. *He has the eyes of a weasel*, Tabitha thought. Greasy bits of meat stuck in his beard.

"Now, small girl," he whispered, "you will come with me and make me a profit!"

Tabitha had backed all the way to the edge of the Sea of Death now. She felt the water wash over her feet, and wondered if the sea or the man would kill her first. Suddenly she decided that she wasn't going to let *either* of them get her. Reaching to the pebbled earth, she picked up a smooth stone larger than her hand. She drew her arm back and threw the rock as hard as if she were trying to kill a lion. The stone hit the man in the elbow and he howled in pain.

But it only made him more mad.

Stepping quickly toward Tabitha, he yelled terrible threats, but Tabitha threw another rock, hitting him on the shoulder. Then she began pelting him with the stones, firing as rapidly as she could. The rocks hit the man in the knee, and the chest, and the neck. Finally a stone hit the man square on his ear and he dropped to the ground, holding his head in his arms. Deciding it was a good time to run, Tabitha slipped on her sandal and dashed off up the beach.

When she'd run as far as her breath would allow, Tabitha dropped down behind a large rock. Forcing herself to gasp for breath quietly, she listened for any sound of footsteps. Hearing nothing for a time, she decided it was safe.

And that's when the tears came.

Tabitha sobbed—as quietly as she could—into the folds of her tunic. She cried at the loss of her father, cried at the cruelty of the Romans, and cried out her fear of the attack in the night.

It was some time later that Tabitha decided she needed to start walking. She had no blanket, and the night air coming off the sea was chilled. And better to be on the road at night, she thought, than during the day when she might meet others. So she started off, the sea on her right, to the place of the monks.

Holding her arms tightly around herself for warmth, Tabitha walked on through the night. The moon was out, though only a third part of it shone with light. But it was enough to see by, and enough to tell that no dangers awaited ahead.

All through the night Tabitha walked. Her legs began to ache after a time, but she didn't even notice enough to complain to herself. She had no water, and thirst scratched at her throat as she walked. But neither aching legs nor a dry mouth were new to her, and she didn't allow these discomforts to slow her down.

Toward morning, Tabitha was finding it difficult to keep her eyes open. She kept telling her eyelids to obey, but they would not. Several times she stumbled and almost fell to the ground as sleep took over her mind. Yet she still continued trudging ahead, one foot in front of the other, not knowing where she was going but knowing she had to go there nonetheless.

The sun had just peeked over the Sea of Death to her right when Tabitha stopped dead in her tracks, her eyes forgetting all about being sleepy. To her left, and a short distance off the road, was a walled compound. At least it *used* to be a walled compound. This wall was nothing but burned rubble in several places, and it didn't even have a proper gate.

It must be Qumran, Tabitha decided.

Slipping down behind some rocks, Tabitha sat and thought. Her father had said that girls weren't allowed in Qumran, and yet she had to go there to find help. How could she get inside the gate and find help when they wouldn't let her in because she was a . . .

Remembering En Gedi, an idea flew into Tabitha's head. Immediately she took the cloth Hasbah had given her and folded it into the shape worn by boys. Then she once again stuffed all her hair up under the hat, and pulled it down tightly so it wouldn't fall off. Next she rubbed some dirt on her face because boys are always dirty. *Boys think they're superior to everyone*, she thought, *so I must have that same attitude if my plan is to work*. She stood and practiced taking long steps, the way boys do, folding her arms in front of her.

The sun was fully awake now, and Tabitha climbed back up on the road and then up a trail toward what looked like the main gate of Qumran. As she did so, she heard a shout, and then saw a man standing in a tower where the walls met in a corner. The man was pointing at her and shouting to someone behind him. He turned and stared at her as she approached, then finally turned away again. This time she heard the words he spoke to those behind him. "All is well," the man was saying.

Tabitha continued on to the gate, and was met by one short, round man and one tall, thin one. "What is it you want?" the short man said gruffly.

Tabitha swallowed hard. She had expected a kinder greeting. Lowering her voice just a touch, she answered, "My father has been arrested by the Romans, and I seek help in freeing him."

"There is no one here who can help you, boy," the short man said with a wave of his hand. "We are monks and do not get involved in such matters. Now away with you, off to Jericho or such."

Tabitha was beginning to panic, and forgot to lower her voice when she spoke. "But my father said I should come here for help! He said to look for a monk playing the part of a fool!"

The little fat man looked up at his friend and said in disgust, "Nathan!" Shaking his head he said, "Very well. The one you seek is not here, but you may wait for him a day or two." And then, wagging his finger in Tabitha's face, he added, "But no longer!" The man turned then, and looked across the compound. Finally he spotted a boy about Tabitha's age and yelled, "Bartholomew!" The boy ran over, skidding to a stop next to the fat man.

"Yes, Rabbi," the boy said, and Tabitha could not believe the mean man was a teacher.

"Take care of this boy! He waits for Nathan. Make sure he knows our rules."

"Yes, Rabbi," the boy said again, and then the two men turned and stomped off. Tabitha was disappointed—she wanted to ask the Rabbi about the fool. But it would have to wait until later, she decided. Until he was in a better mood.

"My name is Bartholomew," the boy said. "And what is your name?"

"Tab—" Tabitha caught herself just in time, and had to think quickly. "Tabaliah," she said, giving a common boy's name.

As they walked through the compound, Bartholomew asked what Tabitha was doing all alone in the desert, and she told him how her father and uncles were arrested by Romans looking for a fool and a boy. Her new friend became silent after that, but Tabitha didn't ask why. Finally he said, "Tabaliah, I am the boy they were looking for. I was rescued from death by my friend Nathan, who often plays the part of a fool." Bartholomew looked Tabitha in the eye and added, "Your father was arrested because of me."

Tabitha was quiet a moment, then said, "My father was arrested because of the Romans, not because of you. Do not feel badly for that which you could not control."

Bartholomew nodded, then began teaching Tabitha the many rules of Qumran, all the while believing she was a boy. This made Tabitha feel guilty. Bartholomew had been honest with her about his role in her father's arrest. But she dared not reveal her true identity for fear she would be pushed out into the desert.

All that changed a few minutes later, when Bartholomew was explaining about meals. "There are only two meals a day here," he said. "But the worst part is, we all have to bathe before every meal!"

"You bathe together?" Tabitha gasped.

"Yes," Bartholomew said. "But it is alright. There are no women or girls here."

Tabitha now knew she could keep quiet no longer. "Bartholomew," she said, "I have a secret I must tell you!"

Tabitha has been hiding her true identity from her new friend. Even though Bartholomew has been honest with her, up until now she felt like she had to pretend to be someone else.

We are often like that ourselves, especially when it comes to letting others know we love Jesus. Sometimes we're afraid we'll be laughed at if our friends know we're Christians. So it's easier to hide our true identities and pretend not to know Jesus.

But God can only use us and bless us when we are open and honest about our relationship with him. As the story in Acts goes,

> When they saw the courage of Peter and John and realized that they were un-
> schooled, ordinary men, they were astonished and they took note that these
> men had been with Jesus. ACTS 4:13

Unless it's a game everyone is playing together, hiding is never any fun. In fact, it can be kind of scary. Wouldn't it be better, and wouldn't it be nice, if everyone just knew you were a Christian? Then people could look at the way you love others and say, "This person has been with Jesus!"

Bartholomew

Light the first two violet candles.

Tabitha wondered if Bartholomew was still breathing. She had pulled him over into the shadows of a building and released her long hair from its covering. "Bartholomew, I am a girl!" she had said. Since then, Bartholomew had stared at her without moving. Finally, he blinked.

"My name is really Tabitha," she said now. "My father, Eliakim, and I were searching for a boy when the Romans stopped us."

Bartholomew continued to stare. "You're . . . you're a *girl!*" he said.

"Yes," Tabitha answered. "And it would be most embarrassing if I had to take a bath with everyone else!"

Bartholomew shook his head to clear it, then stopped and stared again. "You said you search for a boy," he said. "Why?"

"My father put the boy on a caravan," she answered, "and only later found out it was a caravan of thieves, led by an evil man."

"Decha of Megiddo!" Bartholomew said, spitting out the name.

"Yes! How did you know?"

"The boy you searched for," Bartholomew said quickly, "was his name Jotham?"

"Yes!" Tabitha almost screamed, in her excitement. "How did you know?!"

"Because he was here not two days ago!"

"Jotham was here! But what of the fool?"

"My friend Nathan rescued Jotham from Decha," Bartholomew said. "He sometimes dresses as a fool so people don't think him a threat. He and Jotham left yesterday for Jericho."

Tabitha sat back and stared. "Jotham is safe!" she whispered to herself. A moment later she turned to her new friend. "Then there was no need for my father to try finding Jotham! He could have stayed at home and never been bothered by the Romans!"

"Yes," Bartholomew said in a matter-of-fact way, "but you had no way to know that."

Tabitha nodded, and they began talking about Jotham.

"He is a most wondrous friend," Bartholomew said, and Tabitha agreed.

"I think the three of us could all be good friends together," she said.

Tabitha stuffed her hair back under her head covering, then Bartholomew continued showing her around the compound, keeping her clear of the Rabbi.

"Why is the Rabbi so cruel?" she asked.

Bartholomew shook his head. "I do not know. He seems to care a great deal about people, but he doesn't like us boys being here. I guess he thinks we're an interruption to the monks' work."

"And what is their work?" Tabitha asked.

"They make copies of the Torah."

"And do you help?"

"Not with the scrolls," Bartholomew answered. "But I do help make the urns they are stored in. I carry them from the pottery room to the storeroom."

Tabitha thought Bartholomew must be very strong to carry such heavy urns. "And why are you at Qumran?" she asked.

Bartholomew was quiet for a moment, then answered, "The Romans attacked my town and killed many people. I was taken to Caesarea and sold as a slave, while my family was taken on a ship to Rome." He was quiet for another moment, then said, "I think I shall never see them again."

Tabitha knew exactly how he felt. She was beginning to feel like she would never see her father again, or any of her family. They were all so far away, toward the west.

They both sat and thought for a long moment, then Bartholomew said, "You cannot stay here. The Rabbi will surely discover your secret and be angry."

Tabitha nodded her head. "Yes, I know this. But I do not know what else to do. Where can I go?"

Bartholomew had already figured that out. "Nathan and Jotham left just yesterday, so if you hurry you can catch them at the house of Silas in Jericho."

"The house of who?"

"Of Silas," Bartholomew repeated. "He is a most wonderful man of great hospitality. Nathan and I stayed a night with him when we traveled through Jericho."

"How will I find his house?" Tabitha asked. "And how do I find Jericho?"

"Jericho is just a day's walk to the north," Bartholomew answered. "If you leave now, you will be there tomorrow, and only have to spend one night alone. Once you get to Jericho, look for the seller of perfumes . . ."

Bartholomew drew a map of Jericho in the sand, showing Tabitha just how to get to Silas's house. "At the house of Silas," Bartholomew concluded, "you will be safe. Nathan will know how to help you find your family, and save your father."

Tabitha nodded, but was still worried. "Even a day's walk is a long distance for a girl—or boy—alone on a busy road," she said.

Bartholomew nodded, then said, "But you will not be alone. Jehovah will be with you!"

The idea that the God of all things would take the time to walk with a girl had never found Tabitha's head before. "Do you think he would?" Tabitha asked.

"Most assuredly!" Bartholomew answered. "Many times since the Romans attacked my town, I have been in dangerous situations. And every time, Jehovah has rescued me." He thought for a moment more, then added, "I think maybe it is what he does best!"

This made Tabitha feel much better. "If Jehovah is with me," she said with confidence, "I can do *any*thing!"

Bartholomew led Tabitha over to a building where the monks ate their meals. Once inside, they went to the kitchen and talked to an old, gruff-looking man. "My friend Tabaliah must travel to Jericho," he told the cook. "Could you prepare a meal for his travels?"

The cook looked at Tabitha through suspicious eyes. "He must first go outside and bathe," the monk said, and Tabitha's eyes grew wide. But Bartholomew didn't hesitate for a moment, and stepped right in as if he'd known this was going to happen.

"Oh, he is not going to eat the meal now," Bartholomew said. "He will save it for evening. And then, before he eats, he will bathe in the river Jordan."

The cook eyed Tabitha again, and Tabitha nodded her head quickly to confirm Bartholomew's story. "Very well," he said finally, and put some bread and dried meat in a goatskin bag. Bartholomew grabbed a skin of water as well, and a blanket from his dormitory, then led Tabitha out the front gate, where men and boys were busy rebuilding the walls of the compound.

"So go straight north from here along the road," he told his new friend. "And when you get to the house of Silas, greet my friends Nathan and Jotham for me."

Tabitha gave Bartholomew a quick hug. "You are a good friend," she said. "When I find my father and Jotham, I will tell them of your kindness." Then she turned her back on Qumran and began walking up the road, wondering what dangers lay around the next bend.

How terrifying it must be for Tabitha! All alone, walking a strange and dangerous road to a distant and unknown city. She has every right to be afraid!

But Bartholomew is a wise friend. He knows that we are never really alone if God is our friend. Even in the dark of the night, even when there's no one else around, even when we don't know what to do, Jesus is right there with us, walking beside us, holding our hands.

> Do not be afraid or terrified . . . for the Lord your God goes with you; he will never leave you nor forsake you. DEUTERONOMY 31:6

That's a promise God made long ago, and a promise he has always kept.

Serpents

Light the first two violet candles.

At first Tabitha's walking had seemed like an adventure. It was fun to think of Jehovah walking by her side, protecting her from thieves and rascals. But then weariness began to set in, and all her mind would think of was her father. Jerusalem seemed so far away. How would she ever get there? And how would she get the parchment he needed to prove his citizenship?

Thoughts such as these were only interrupted by the occasional traveler on the road. As she had planned with Bartholomew, every time she saw someone approaching, she hid behind a eucalyptus tree or a large rock or in the bed of a dried-up wadi. The last such traveler she had seen was a man riding a horse at terrifying speed, headed toward Qumran. The man was wearing the same tunics as the monks there, and had a look of terrible fright on his face. Tabitha wondered if he carried some awful message to Qumran, but decided she would never know the answer to that question.

Since then, Tabitha's walking had become very boring. It was no longer an adventure, but simply a matter of putting one foot in front of the other. Then she heard the hooves of horses approaching from the direction of Jericho, and once again scrambled to the side of the road. Hiding behind a thorny bush, she looked up at the road above her and saw five men on horses riding hard and fast.

And in the lead was Decha of Megiddo.

Tabitha had only seen him once, when Jotham had joined his caravan. But his coat of many colors could not be mistaken for any other. The sight of the man made her ribs tremble, and she had to bite her lip to keep from screaming.

But Decha and his men were riding fast, and could not see the girl behind the thornbush. A moment later they had passed by in a cloud of dust.

It took Tabitha several minutes to make herself come out of hiding. Seeing Decha had scared her so that sitting behind a thornbush for the rest of all time seemed like a good idea. But then she took a deep breath, forced herself to stand, and said out loud, "Tabitha, Jehovah is with you! And besides, Decha was going the other direction."

With that she stepped back onto the road and continued her travels. The only difference was that every bit of boredom had left her.

The rest of the afternoon wore on with no more frights, and when the sun began to drop behind the hills, Tabitha made a camp for herself by the waters of the Sea of Death. She still wouldn't drink those waters, of course, because everyone knows they are poison. But just hearing the water lapping on the shore was comforting, as if there was something alive to keep her company.

After building a small fire and laying out the blanket Bartholomew had given her, Tabitha ate her supper of bread and dried lamb. She giggled at the thought that perhaps she should have taken a bath before eating, and it felt good to have humor in her day again.

A short while later, just as her eyelids were getting heavy and sleep was approaching on the breeze, she heard footsteps.

Horses! Horses approaching! In a flash, Tabitha scrambled away from the fire and out into the darkness of the night. Finding another empty wadi in the dark, she slid down its banks until she could just see over the top of it, and looked toward her camp.

And there, by her fire, stood Decha of Megiddo.

Tabitha shivered, partly because it had turned bitterly cold by now, but partly at the sight of the thief. Decha was surrounded by the four other men on horses. He kicked at Tabitha's blanket, ran his toe around the edge of her fire. Suddenly he looked up, directly toward her, and she ducked down into the wadi. *He could not have seen me*, she thought, *but maybe he heard me.*

Tabitha forced herself to slow her breathing, and to not wiggle so much as a toe lest she dislodge a pebble or snap a twig. For many long breaths she heard nothing, but then there was laughter—cruel laughter, such as one might hear from an insane man. She raised her head up slowly and peeked over the top of the wadi once more. Decha and his men were seated around the fire, with Decha seated on the blanket given to her by Bartholomew. Tabitha slid back down the wall of the wadi and lay her head against the dirt. *Why is this happening?* she asked silently. *Isn't Jehovah here to take care of me? Doesn't he care?*

Such thoughts ran through Tabitha's mind several times, then she caught herself and decided that whining—even silently—wasn't going to help. She needed a plan.

First she considered just leaving for Jericho and finding her way in the dark. She had done it the night before, so she could probably do it again. But then she realized that she hadn't slept all day, and in fact hadn't been asleep since her father was arrested. Suddenly Tabitha's eyelids became very heavy, and she felt as though she were about to fall into a deep canyon . . .

Tabitha shook her head. *I must stay awake*, she thought. *At least until I am someplace safe*. But where could that be? Without her blanket she would die of the cold if she fell asleep. But she couldn't exactly walk up to Decha and ask him for it. So how could she get her blanket in such a way that Decha . . .

Suddenly an idea introduced itself in Tabitha's head. She greeted it, became familiar with it, liked it a lot, and could find no fault in it. *Jehovah,* she prayed, *I put my faith in you. I trust you to give me the wisdom and courage to survive this night!* Feeling that God really was with her, she slid down to the bed of the wadi and began to crawl. When she thought she was far enough away that small noises wouldn't be heard, she rose to her feet and climbed up the wall of the dried-up streambed. Now she could see her fire in the distance, and could judge how to proceed.

Walking ever so slowly, Tabitha was careful with every footstep so as not to make a sound. Closer and closer she walked toward the camp, the ground just visible in the light of the partial moon. Soon she could hear the men talking—rough talk, ugly talk. Talk such as her father and uncles never made. Then she could smell the horses, and knew which way her path should turn. Now she could see the faces of the men in the firelight, and knew that because of that light, they would not be able to see her.

Another step closer, then another, until Tabitha thought her insides might shiver right out of her body from fear. She was so close now that she thought she could probably count the whiskers on Decha's chin if she wanted. Just out of range of the firelight, she slowly worked her way over to the horses. Moving up between two of the animals, she patted them on the sides so as not to spook them.

The horses were all tied to the same eucalyptus tree, and had eaten off its lowest branches. Pulling the loops of the knots apart, she freed the ropes one by one until all five horses were held by nothing more than their own belief that they were still tied.

Stepping backward as silently as she had come forward, Tabitha moved slowly away from the camp again. Her plan needed one more thing, and she thought she knew just where to find it. Watching as carefully as she could in the moonlight, she crept over to a pile of rocks that had slid down a hillside. There, warming itself on a stone that had been heated all day in the sun, was a snake as long as she was tall.

Tabitha knew the dangers of playing with snakes, but she had learned from her brothers how to safely handle them. Slowly, she reached in over the rock, and grabbed the asp behind the head.

Instantly the reptile started writhing and jerking, but Tabitha held tightly. Moving more quickly now, and anxious to get rid of her new pet, she silently moved back up behind the horses. With a mighty swing of her arm, she threw the snake into the middle of the beasts. Three of the horses saw the slithering creature and reared up. With frightened whinnies blasting through the night, the horses suddenly realized they were no longer tied up, and took off into the desert night. The other two didn't see the snake, but followed the lead of their three companions and ran off as well.

Decha and his men had jumped to their feet at the first sound from the frightened horses. They looked to where the horses had been securely tied a moment before. And the cold fingers of fear tickled Tabitha's spine when Decha stared her straight in the eye.

Having faith that God will do what he promised is kind of hard for us humans. We like to be in control of our own lives. We like to make things happen for ourselves.

But when times are really tough, and it seems impossible to escape, having practiced our faith beforehand makes it easier to believe.

Tabitha has trusted God for many things these past several days. Now she's ready to trust him for one big thing.

> Let us fix our eyes on Jesus, the author and perfecter of our faith, who for the joy set before him endured the cross, scorning its shame, and sat down at the right hand of the throne of God.   HEBREWS 12:2

Ask Jesus for the gift of faith this Christmas. Not only faith that he will take care of you, but faith that he truly has made a place for you in heaven, as well.

Jericho

Light the first two violet candles.

Tabitha froze in place, too scared even to breathe. Decha stared straight at her from twenty paces away. In her planning, she had thought the night to be dark enough that she could hide, especially since the five thieves had been staring into the fire. Everyone knows, she had thought, that you can't see well in the dark if you've been looking at the light.

But now Tabitha knew she was wrong. Decha *could* see, and he was seeing *her* right now! A moment later Decha motioned with his arm and yelled to his men, "Follow me!" Some part of Tabitha knew that she should run, but her legs would not obey. She stood frozen in place, eyes wide, staring at Decha charging right at her. Decha's men fanned out on either side, surrounding Tabitha like a fish in a net.

But then a strange thing happened: Decha went right past Tabitha, a few paces to her left. She waited for the blow from behind, but the men just kept running. Finally, Tabitha turned slowly, just in time to see all five of the thieves chasing their horses into the night. *My plan worked!* she realized suddenly. Breaking her feet loose from the grip of fear, she ran toward the campfire, scooped up the blanket without even stopping, and dashed off into the night.

Angling up toward the roadway, Tabitha ran faster than she ever had before—faster even than her brothers chasing a rabbit. Around a bend in the road, and then another, she ran until her lungs were filled with fire and her throat felt like the sand under her feet. When the last stride finally left her legs and there were no more to be found, she collapsed by the side of the road, heaving in great gasps of air like a horse after a race.

Slowly, Tabitha's breathing eased and her shaking calmed. She listened carefully for any sound of foot or hoof searching for her, but heard none. Confident that she would not be found, she lay down behind a juniper bush, wrapped the soft blanket around her, and fell asleep for the first time in two days.

Tabitha was shocked to see her caravan approaching. Led by her uncle Ananias, with her mother just behind him, the long stream of camels, donkeys, sheep, and people was lumbering up the road from En Gedi. And there, right in the middle of it, was her father!

"Father, Father!" Tabitha cried, as she ran toward him. Her father smiled and waved, and Tabitha felt as if the whole world had started moving again after a long pause. But no matter how fast Tabitha ran, she couldn't catch up with her family. She ran and ran and ran, but they kept getting farther away. Soon the last of the sheep had passed by on the road, and still she could not catch them. A moment later, they were gone, around the next bend in the road.

"Stop!" she called after them, crying. "Wait!" But they neither stopped nor waited. Once again, Tabitha was all alone in the desert.

And that's when she woke up.

Flies swarmed around Tabitha's head and she brushed them away. The sun was high in the sky, and she was sweating under the warm blanket. She blinked several times to wake up. The caravan, her family—it was only a dream. This realization made her very sad, sadder than she'd ever been in her entire life.

It's like I'm on one side of Palestine, she thought, *and my whole family is clear on the other side!* A moment later she realized that was exactly the case, and that thought made the pain in her heart even worse.

I lift up my eyes to the hills . . . The verse from the Psalms that she had used to comfort her father now came to comfort *her*. *Fear not*, the words in her head continued, *for I am with you*. As if she had been wrapped in another blanket, a blanket of love, Tabitha felt like Jehovah truly was with her, sitting beside her in the desert, ready to comfort and protect her.

"And he already has," Tabitha said out loud as she thought about her raid on "Decha's" camp the night before. Remembering how she had sneaked up between the horses and freed them, how she had captured the serpent and used it to frighten the beasts, how Decha had seemed to run right at her but couldn't see her because she stood perfectly still . . . Tabitha's mouth dropped open and she stared out toward the sea. "*I did all that?!*" she whispered to the wind. Then she realized it was not in her own strength that she had done these things. "Jehovah, you truly are with me!" she said after a moment. "And now I know you will take care of me no matter what!"

With that, Tabitha stood, folded her blanket, and set out up the road toward Jericho. Along the way she found a fig tree that had not been picked clean by other travelers. *How strange,* she thought as she filled her belly with the fruit, *that the many people who pass by this tree have ignored these few figs. And just enough for my breakfast!*

The sun was straight overhead now, and Tabitha continued her walk. As the sun traveled across the sky, Tabitha traveled along the road. She was passed by only two other bands of wanderers, and both times she hid until they were far down the road. At about the time her stomach was telling her it was ready for dinner, Tabitha came around a bend and saw the most wondrous sight she had seen in days. There, before her, surrounded by green palm trees and a rainbow of fruit, sat the glowing city of Jericho.

I made it! Tabitha wanted to cheer. *But I must not look like a lost little girl; I must look like I belong here!* Tabitha shook her head and wondered where *that* thought had come from. But she saw the wisdom in it, and looked around for something to help her. There, lying alongside the road as if it had been placed there just for her, was a small urn. She picked up the vessel, wondering why someone would leave a perfectly good pot by the side of the road. Then she saw a tiny crack in it, and knew it had been thrown away.

Satisfied that she was not stealing something somebody had simply lost, Tabitha tied her blanket around her waist, held the urn in her arms, and walked into Jericho as if she knew exactly what she was doing and where she was going. The problem was that neither of these was true. She *wanted* to stop and gawk at all the sellers from foreign lands, and the makers of jewelry and perfumes and clothes. But she dared not look interested lest someone recognize that she was all alone, without a parent in close attendance. Such knowledge would give a kidnapper great courage, she knew.

Pushing her way down the crowded main street, Tabitha tried to look for the landmarks Bartholomew had drawn for her in the sand. She was getting excited now, knowing that, within a few minutes, she'd be celebrating with Jotham, and his new friends Nathan and

Silas. As she passed through the delightful smells from the seller of cheese, she imagined how good it would feel to hug her friend, and to see a familiar face. Bartholomew had assured her that Nathan and Silas would do everything necessary to help her find her father and prove his Roman citizenship. All these imaginings made Tabitha so happy that she walked even faster, anxious now to get to her destination.

A potter! Bartholomew had said to turn right at the first potter's shop she saw, and there it was. The side street was not nearly as crowded, and Tabitha passed children playing and women humming songs as they hung clothes to dry. It was indeed a happy place, a safe place.

Look for two palm trees by a well, Bartholomew had told her, and turn left. The house of Silas is the first house on the corner on the right. *Two palm trees!* Tabitha cried to herself when she saw them. She was getting so close now that she didn't care if she looked lost or not. She ran ahead, dragging the little urn by the rim. Then she saw the well at the base of the trees and knew the house of Silas was just around the corner. Past women drawing water, she ran, through a group of children playing camel races. With the sound of her clapping sandals echoing off the walls of the buildings, she ran the last few lengths down to the corner of the next street on the left.

And there she stopped and stared, stunned. The house of Silas stood open and empty. Inside she could see that thieves had ransacked the house, and left little behind but broken pottery and piles of trash. A moment later snakes ran up her spine as a bony hand gripped her shoulder and Tabitha heard a man's hissing voice whisper in her ear, "Are you lost, little girl?"

"Reversal of fortune" is a phrase writers use to describe the moment their hero goes from being safe and secure to being in utter peril. Sometimes our "fortunes" are reversed in real life, as well. Everything seems to be going along fine, then *wham*, a tragedy hits, and it seems as if life itself will never be the same.

The question isn't whether or not those reversals will happen in our lives. The question is, what will we *do* when they happen?

I lift up my eyes to the hills—where does my help come from? My help comes from the LORD, the Maker of heaven and earth.   PSALM 121:1–2

Tabitha comforted her father with these words early in her adventure. She uses them now to comfort herself. As Christmas approaches, perhaps they are good words for us to learn, and memorize, and believe, to prepare us for the "reversals of fortune" that might lie ahead.

The Star

Light the first two violet candles.

Tabitha struggled to free herself from the man's grip, but he held her tightly. She spun around and saw that he had only two teeth, and both were black with rot. His eyes were red and his nose crooked. His lips pulled back in what Tabitha thought was supposed to be a grin, but was lopsided and evil. With drool running from his mouth, the man said, "Come with me, and I'll help you find your way!"

"No!" Tabitha yelled, still struggling. "Let *go* of me!" But still the man hung on.

"I thinks you will fetch a fine price," the man hissed, and he started to lift her under his arm to carry her. But before her feet even left the ground, Tabitha decided she was not going to be someone's slave girl. With all her strength she swung the pot in her hand and hit the man square on the head. The pot shattered, the man screamed, and Tabitha broke free.

Having no idea what else to do, Tabitha ran into the house of Silas. "Jotham!" she yelled. "Nathan! Silas!" But no one answered. Everywhere she looked she found only rubble and charred remains in the once beautiful house.

Tabitha heard a moan and looked back toward the street. Her attacker had fallen to the ground, but was now struggling to his knees. In moments he would be standing again, and very angry. Without another thought and with no plan other than to get away, she ran out a side door of the house and down a winding street. At the next corner she turned left, onto a wider street, and tried to hide herself among the crowds of people. She was just starting to catch her breath, and to wonder what she would do now, when she saw a wonderful sight: her grandmother's donkey, the one she had given to Jotham, tied outside a shop of spices.

Tabitha's heart soared with hope. She ran to the donkey and greeted it like an old friend.

"Elisha!" she yelled. "How I have missed you!" She gave the donkey a kiss on the nose, then said, "And where is your new master?" She looked around, trying to see Jotham amidst all the travelers and sellers and children. But he was nowhere to be seen. Then she noticed that the strap holding the donkey's saddle in place was tied wrong, and was cutting into the beast's flesh. "You poor animal!" Tabitha cried. "How could Jotham let you suffer so?" She loosened the strap, and was just starting to retie it, when she heard a screeching cackle like a beast in her worst nightmares.

"Don't you touch my donkey!" a haggard old woman screamed. The woman waddled like a big duck as she ran, and was shaking a bony finger at Tabitha. "Get away, girl! Or I'll sell you to my son for a profit!"

Tabitha stood up straight and stood her ground. "This is *not* your donkey," she said as the woman reached her. *She looks like a witch*, Tabitha thought, eyeing her ragged clothes adorned with cheap bracelets and pins. *And she smells like one too!*

"It *is* my donkey, and I'll beat you like a dog if you don't back away!" The woman was waving a wooden walking stick over her head, and Tabitha decided that perhaps this wasn't the best time to be brave.

"I'm going to go find the real owner of this animal," Tabitha said, "and then we're coming back here to have you arrested!"

The old woman stopped swinging the stick around, and looked Tabitha straight in the eye. "The one who owned this donkey before me," she growled, "was a boy of ten. But he is dead now, and the donkey is *mine!*"

Tabitha stumbled backward. Her mouth opened and closed but no sound would come out. *Jotham, dead? How . . . when . . . why . . . ?* Questions and feelings stumbled around inside her head. Her thoughts were all mixed up like rats in a whirlpool. Tabitha turned away from the witch, and out into the street. *Jotham, dead?* she kept thinking. What would she do now?

Tabitha wandered through the streets, not even noticing the colorful people and strange wares. Images of Silas's deserted house kept forcing their way into her head, and she wondered if Jotham had been inside when it was looted. Finally she spotted an inn, and remembered the fine meal she had shared with her father at such a place. Pushing through the door, she sat on a bench just inside and put her head in her hands.

"No begging here!" came a gruff voice from the other side of the room. "And no peddling either! Go your way, and don't bother my guests."

Tabitha looked up and saw several people at tables around the inn, all of them staring at her.

"I come neither to beg nor to peddle," she said wearily. "I come only to rest, and perhaps have a drink of water." She stopped for a moment, hoping for an invitation, but none came. "Very well, I will go," she said, and stood to her feet.

"Hold!" came the voice, though not quite so gruffly. "If water is all you seek, I can spare a cup." The man came over to Tabitha then, carrying a ladle of water. He was tall and thin, with a thin, narrow beard. Tabitha gulped down the water and thanked him.

"And where is your family?" the man asked. Tabitha's lonely heart poured out the answer to that question, starting with finding a boy in the desert. A large cockroach made four trips clear across the room and back, carrying crumbs of bread with each pass, in the time it took Tabitha to tell her story.

"This boy," the man said when she had finished, "could it be that his name is Jotham of Jericho?"

Tabitha's eyes shot open. "Yes!" she exclaimed. But then sadness took over once again as she added, "But he is dead now."

"Dead! When did this happen? How did he die?"

"I do not know. It was told me by an old woman who had his donkey," Tabitha said.

The man made a disgusted, snorting sound and waved his hand. "That old witch is the mother of Decha of Megiddo," he said. "She lies worse than her son! Jotham is very well and alive, and is even now in the company of a priest to the north!"

"Are you sure?" Tabitha gasped.

"By my honor!" the man answered. Then he sat down next to her to tell his story. "My name is Seth," he began, "and I was a friend to Silas. A very good friend. I watched him die right here on this floor," he said, closing his eyes from the pain of the memory. "Jotham was here too, and his friend Nathan." Seth was quiet for a long moment, and Tabitha dared not interrupt his thinkings. Then he shook his head and continued.

"I heard Nathan tell another man—a fellow innkeeper—to take the boy to a priest in the north while he himself stayed to fight Decha. Hasrah was the man's name, Hasrah of Bethlehem. He didn't want to leave the fight, but followed the bidding of Nathan. He ran out the door in back with the boy under his arm. I and some other men in the inn joined the battle and scared Decha off, but by then, Jotham and Hasrah were far away."

Tabitha took all this in for several moments, then asked, "Where is Nathan now?"

Seth shook his head sadly. "He went off into the hills on foot to follow the boy."

They sat in silence for a time, then Seth slapped both his knees at once and said, "But now it is time to work. You may stay here as long as you wish, and have a bed and your meals free of charge. I do this to honor my friend Silas, and his friend Jotham."

Tabitha thanked Seth, and felt like she finally had a friend again.

But later that night, as she lay on a bedroll in the dark, staring out a window, Tabitha thought of her family. "Jehovah," she prayed, "please help me find my father! Please lead me to him before the Romans kill him!"

Suddenly a bright light filled Tabitha's eyes, and a star which shone like no other filled the sky. Tabitha rushed to the door and out into the street. She stared into the sky, taking in the wondrous sight, until at last the thought of a thing she must do had fully arrived in her head.

Running back inside the inn, Tabitha shook her sleeping host and whispered in his ear. "Seth!" she said, "wake up! I must leave this place at once!"

Lies are the native language of the devil. If we listen to those lies, they will hurt us, make our lives miserable, and make it difficult for us to see God.

But Jesus came to earth to show us the truth—so we can know the one true God:

> Jesus answered, "I am the way and the truth and the life. No one comes to the Father except through me. If you really knew me, you would know my Father as well. From now on, you do know him and have seen him."   JOHN 14:6–7

You may think Christmas is just about Jesus' birth. But it is much more than that. It's about knowing God, and knowing the truth, as well.

Tabitha had her friend Seth to explain that she was listening to lies. Wouldn't Christmas be a good time to let *your* friends know the truth about *God*?

The Priest

Light the first two violet candles.

Seth forced one eye open and whispered, "Girl! What is it?"

"We must leave at once!" Tabitha answered.

"Leave?" the innkeeper mumbled. "Why would we want to leave?"

"I have seen it in the sky! Jehovah is calling to me!"

Seth had both eyes halfway opened now, and sat up on his sleeping mat. He shook his head slowly, then sighed. "Show me this thing in the sky," he said.

Stepping carefully around the sleeping bodies of the guests, Tabitha led Seth out through the front door and into the street. Seth looked up at the strange star in the sky and gasped. "What is this?" he cried.

Tabitha was also craning her neck to see the star. "I prayed to Jehovah for his help," she said, "and this star appeared. I did not think he would answer my prayers so quickly!"

Seth just stared at the sight, his mouth hanging open. "I do not know if Jehovah answers the prayers of small girls," he said, "but this star truly is a miracle! We must follow it, and see where it leads!"

Tabitha had scowled at Seth's lack of faith, but now grinned at his agreement to travel with her. Seth woke his wife and explained what was going on, and though she accepted the news quietly, she didn't seem pleased. Then Seth packed a bag with some food and water, grabbed a couple of blankets, and led Tabitha out the back door. There he unhitched a camel that looked to Tabitha like an old, worn-out rug. Seth clicked his tongue and the camel lowered himself unsteadily to the ground. They climbed atop and then, with another click of Seth's tongue, the animal lurched to his feet and they headed up the streets of Jericho.

Once outside the city, Seth kicked his heels and the camel trotted down the roadway. "Where are we going?" Tabitha asked at last.

"I do not know," Seth answered. "I only follow the star!" He pointed to the sky and added, "It seems to be drawing us toward the west."

"Toward Jerusalem?" Tabitha gasped, knowing that's where the Romans took her father.

Seth shook his head. "I do not know. If it wants to take us to Jerusalem, this is a strange path to lead us. There is a very fine road to the north of Jericho."

Tabitha wondered what all that meant, but was too sleepy to put her thoughts into order. Sitting in front of Seth, her head began to nod, and even before Seth had turned the camel to the right and headed off the road up into the hills, Tabitha was sound asleep.

She awoke hours later, as the sun was edging up over the hill they had climbed in the night. Tabitha blinked several times, trying to figure out what she was doing on a smelly old camel, then finally remembered.

"Where are we?" she asked, rubbing her eyes and yawning.

"I do not know," Seth answered. Tabitha spun her head around and looked him in the eye. "You don't know where we are!"

Seth shook his head. "No. I rarely leave Jericho, and have never been in these hills."

"Then why are we here?"

Seth shrugged his shoulders. "I only followed the star," he said. "I did not ask it where it was taking me."

Tabitha had forgotten all about the star, and now looked around the sky to find it, but it was gone. A moment later Seth said, "Perhaps the star was leading us to this compound."

Tabitha spun back around to look straight in front of the camel. There she saw several small buildings, and a barn made of wood. The barn had a corral around it where cows grazed on dew-covered grass. A rooster was crowing to wake up his master, but the master was already there—an old, old man, throwing grain to some chickens. As they approached, the man looked up, and his hand went to the sword hanging at his side.

"Who is that?" he called. "Who's there?"

Seth stopped the camel a safe distance away. "It is Seth, an innkeeper from Jericho, and a small child searching for her father."

The old man relaxed. "*Another* homeless child?" he said, and Tabitha wondered what he meant. "Come then, and rest your bones at our breakfast table."

Seth clicked his tongue and the camel knelt down, allowing the two riders to slide off its back. The old man came forward with his hand extended toward Seth. "I am Zechariah," he said, "a priest in the house of God."

"And I am Seth, a man of no importance, son of no one of fame."

"Jehovah cares not for the fame of your father," the priest said. "You are important to him just as you are." Zechariah turned his attention to Tabitha. "And who is this?" he asked.

"My name is Tabitha."

"Another lost child comes from the night," Zechariah said, shaking his head. "What strange events are taking place these days!"

"What other lost child have you seen?" Tabitha asked.

"A boy of ten, who was separated from his shepherd family."

Tabitha gasped. "Jotham!" she shouted.

"Why, yes," said Zechariah. "How do you know of him?"

A brown mouse made five trips across the compound carrying scraps of food to his den as Tabitha explained about all the adventures that had brought her so far from her family. As she was finishing her story, Zechariah led them both inside where they met his wife, Elizabeth, and sat at a wooden table to eat a breakfast of parched wheat.

"Then I saw a strange star last night," Tabitha concluded, "and it led us here to you."

Zechariah was quiet for a moment, then asked Seth, "By what route did you travel last night?"

Seth's forehead wrinkled up as he thought. "Well, we only followed the star, and it brought us up the ravine near Tolbeth, then by the peaks of Ras Shamra."

Zechariah sighed. "Then you wouldn't have seen Jotham and Nathan. As you were coming up the hill to the south of Jericho, they were going down the hill to the north! They are even now staying at the former house of Silas."

"We missed him?" Tabitha cried. "We were so close!"

"Yes, child," Zechariah said. "But my mind tells me it is not Jotham you need to worry about, but your father."

"This is so," Tabitha said sullenly. "Now that we know Jotham is safe, I must help my father. But still," she sighed, "it would have been nice to see him. Why does he travel back to Jericho?"

So Zechariah told her how Jotham had been kidnapped by Decha, and how Caleb and Nathan had rescued the boy. "And now they are safe in Jericho," he concluded. "As for you," he added, looking at Tabitha, "someone must help you get to Jerusalem immediately!"

The priest turned his gaze to Seth, who said, "My inn is full and my duties many, but I will gladly take the girl where she needs to go."

Zechariah looked at his wife. "As for me, my years are many and my bones are old, but they have a few more journeys to Jerusalem left in them. You go back to your inn, Seth. I shall accompany the girl."

Tabitha wondered if this old man could really keep up with her, but didn't say anything.

Seth bowed and said, "Your kindness will be remembered." He rested a few more minutes, then Tabitha gave him a hug goodbye and he headed off down the hill on his camel.

"Well now, child," Zechariah said when Seth had left. "Do your legs have a good day's walk in them, or must we take donkeys?"

Tabitha thought her legs would probably walk twice as far as his, but only said, "My legs will be happy to make the journey."

"Then give me until noon to tend to my animals and other business, and then we shall leave."

Everything was moving so fast that Tabitha wasn't even sure where she was or who she was with. But she returned to the house and slept on a mat in the kitchen until mid-morning.

"After a long night's journey, your sleep must have felt good," Zechariah's wife, Elizabeth, said when Tabitha awoke.

Tabitha stretched and yawned. "It did indeed!" she said. A baby cried behind her, and Tabitha spun around in surprise. "I did not see a baby here before! Who does it belong to?"

"It is mine," Elizabeth said, as she sewed closed a hole in an old tunic.

Tabitha looked at the woman who was obviously many years older than Tabitha's grandmother had been when she died. "It is your baby?" she asked. And then, with no intention of being rude, she added, "How can that be?"

Elizabeth smiled and kept working. "Come, sit with me," she said, "and I will tell you a most miraculous story!"

Does God really do that? Does he really put stars in the sky to guide us, or perform other miracles to show us the way? Yes, because it's a promise he's made to us:

> I will lead the blind by ways they have not known, along unfamiliar paths
> I will guide them; I will turn the darkness into light before them and make
> the rough places smooth. These are the things I will do; I will not forsake
> them. ISAIAH 42:16

Those who have been faithful to God for a while can probably tell of times when he has miraculously guided them. Maybe not with a star in the sky (although I'm sure that's happened a few times), but in any number of unexpected ways. In fact, when we're wondering how God will guide us in the future, about the only thing we can be sure of is that it will be in a way we never expected, maybe even in a way he's never done before.

Tabitha knew from the moment she saw the star that God was at work. When we look at the manger of Christmas, we know that as well. But if we're faithful in following the path we know God has set for us, there will also be times in our lives when he will guide us in wondrous and miraculous ways we never dreamed of.

Angels

Light two violet candles and the pink candle.

For many years," Elizabeth started her story, sewing even as she spoke, "Zechariah and I prayed to Jehovah for children, but none came to us. Zechariah was a priest all that time, and couldn't understand why his God remained silent."

Tabitha looked on in awe. She was used to hearing stories around the campfire every night, and had missed them these last several days. But those were all the same old stories told over and over. None had ever sounded like this, with people who were still alive!

"Then about two years ago," Elizabeth continued, "Zechariah was on duty in the temple in Jerusalem. It was his job to purify himself, and then enter the Holy Place."

"What is *that*?" Tabitha gasped.

Elizabeth thought for a moment, then said, "The temple is made of several areas, with the most important in the middle. First there is the court of the gentiles, then the court of women, the court of men, and so on."

"You mean men can go farther into the temple than women?" Tabitha exclaimed.

"Yes, child, that is how it must be." The heat of anger rose in Tabitha's cheeks, and she thought to herself that she was every bit as good as any boy, but she kept her lips tightly sealed. "In the very center of the courtyards is the temple itself," Elizabeth continued, "and inside that are two very large rooms. The first is the Holy Place, where the priests daily burn incense and make offerings to God. But at one end of that room is a thick curtain that goes from the floor to the ceiling, and from one wall to the other." Elizabeth stopped sewing and closed her eyes. "Well, it used to be that behind the veil was the ark of the covenant, the golden chest that held the ten laws of God that Moses brought down the mountain, as well as an urn of manna, and the very staff of Aaron. This place . . ." she said in a whisper, and Tabitha had to lean forward to hear her, "this place is the Holy of Holies. The ark was lost to us many years ago, but still it is the most holy place in all the world. Only the high priest may enter the Holy of Holies, and only once each year, on the Day of Atonement."

Tabitha's head was so full of thoughts that she feared they'd all leak out if she didn't finish thinking them. Her first thought was that Zechariah, the old man who was taking her to Jerusalem, had actually been in the house of God! Her second thought was that she'd better stop thinking bad thoughts about Zechariah! And her third thought came out of her mouth: "What happened next?"

The baby cried again, and this time Elizabeth picked him up and cuddled him. "As I said, it was Zechariah's turn to work in the Holy Place. He had been in there a short time when an angel appeared and spoke to him."

"An angel?" Tabitha asked. "What did he say?"

Elizabeth shrugged. "He said, 'Do not be afraid, Zechariah; your prayer has been heard. Your wife Elizabeth will bear you a son, and you are to give him the name John.' Well, of course Zechariah thought this funny, and told the angel so. 'I am an old man,' he said, 'and my wife is well along in years.'"

Tabitha was beginning to understand, and looked at the child in Elizabeth's lap.

"This made the angel angry," Elizabeth continued. "'I am Gabriel,' he said. 'I stand in the presence of God, and I have been sent to speak to you and to tell you this good news. And now you will be silent and not able to speak until the day this happens, because you did not believe my words!' And so Zechariah remained silent. I became pregnant, and gave birth to this fine boy here," she said, holding the baby up to face her. "Eight days after his birth, we took him to the temple to be dedicated to the Lord. My relatives all tried to get us to name the boy after them, but my husband wrote, 'No! His name is John.' At that moment, his tongue was released, and we both praised God for his miracles."

Tabitha sat in silence for a long time, staring at the baby, stunned by the amazing story. Finally she said quietly, reverently, "John. What a beautiful name." She looked from the baby to his mother and added, "And what a wondrous story!"

"Yes, it is," Elizabeth said. "But not nearly as wondrous as the story of my cousin."

"What story?" Tabitha asked. But at just that moment the door opened and Zechariah entered. "I have finished my chores early, and we will leave for Jerusalem immediately."

Tabitha was distressed because she wanted to hear the miraculous story Elizabeth was about to tell. But more than that, she wanted to go find her father. So she gathered her few things, hugged John goodbye, and then hugged Elizabeth.

"Ask Zechariah about my cousin," Elizabeth whispered in Tabitha's ear. "He will pretend he doesn't want to tell it, but just insist. He really likes telling people."

Tabitha grinned at Elizabeth, and held their secret inside her. Then she followed Zechariah out the door and off across the plateau on a narrow trail headed west. Within minutes, Tabitha concluded she'd been completely wrong about the old man. She would have to work hard to keep up with him. Already she was having to breathe heavily to keep her legs moving, but Zechariah acted as if he was out for a leisurely stroll.

"Do I walk too fast for you, child?" Zechariah called back.

"No, not yet," Tabitha huffed. "But you are a very strong walker!"

"I have walked these trails for many years," the old priest answered.

Soon they left the tall, dry grass of the plateau and started down a narrow trail into a sharp canyon. The trail twisted and turned, and Tabitha understood why Zechariah hadn't wanted to bring any animals. Their sure footing would be safer, but they would also travel very slowly. Zechariah was bothered by neither the steepness nor the narrowness of the trail, and as they started climbing the other side of the barren canyon, Tabitha decided he would make a very fine mountain goat. *In fact*, she giggled to herself, *he looks a bit like a mountain goat!*

"What are you giggling at, girl?" Zechariah asked over his shoulder.

"Oh, nothing really," Tabitha answered. "I was just thinking how nice it would be to be a mountain goat right now."

"Ah, yes, I've had that thought many times myself. In fact, my wife has often commented that I *look* much like a mountain goat!"

Tabitha laughed out loud now, and Zechariah turned with a smile. "I see you agree with her!"

"Uh, no! Uh, I mean . . ."

Zechariah laughed. "There is no offense taken."

They reached the top of the hill and Tabitha's heart sank. Before them she saw at least three more steep canyons to be crossed. As far as she could see in the distance, there was nothing but hilltops. Zechariah stopped and pulled out his water pouch. He offered it to Tabitha saying, "Drink lightly, child. There is still far to go."

After a refreshing drink, they started down into the next canyon, and that's when Tabitha finally got up the courage to ask her question.

"Zechariah, Elizabeth told me that God has worked a miraculous wonder in her cousin, but she did not have time to tell me the story. Could you tell me?"

Zechariah harrumphed and shook his head. "I am a priest, not a storyteller," he said crossly.

Tabitha would have quit right there if Elizabeth hadn't warned her of this, but now she plunged ahead. "Pleeeease, Zechariah! I need a good story to keep my mind off the narrow trails and steep canyons."

Zechariah sighed, then said, "Very well, I will tell you the story. But you must not interrupt me!"

"I won't!" Tabitha agreed.

"Very well," Zechariah said again. "It all started the day that Elizabeth's cousin, Mary, came to visit . . ."

Why is God so slow sometimes? It seems to take him *forever* to get things done! Why can't he just work on *our* time schedules—do things when *we're* ready?

Maybe it has something to do with the fact that he's smarter than we are. Maybe he sees things in ways that we don't understand. Perhaps his timing is better than ours.

If God sometimes seems reluctant to answer our prayers and meet our needs, you can be sure it's for good reason. Zechariah became impatient when God didn't give him a son, yet God knew that son would come at just the right time, when it served his purpose.

"For my thoughts are not your thoughts, neither are your ways my ways," declares the LORD. "As the heavens are higher than the earth, so are my ways higher than your ways and my thoughts than your thoughts." ISAIAH 55:8–9

The people of Israel wondered if the Messiah would ever come. Sometimes we have trouble waiting for God to hear our prayers. But as surely as the Messiah *did* come, and as surely as Christmas *will* come, so will God answer our cries for help.

It just might not be in our timing.

Lost Boys

Light two violet candles and the pink candle.

Tabitha picked her way through a field of rocks, fearing she'd twist her ankle at every step. Zechariah had said this would be a shortcut, but Tabitha thought she'd just as soon take the long cut.

As she stepped from one bare spot to another, Tabitha thought about the story Zechariah had just told. Elizabeth's cousin, Mary, was to have a child by the Spirit of God! Angels appearing to Mary and her husband, Joseph! And most amazing of all, the boy whom Mary was to bring into the world will be the Messiah! It was all too much for Tabitha to take in, so she turned her thoughts once again to the endless stones her feet had to battle.

"Are there words for your thoughts?" Zechariah asked. "You have been silent since I finished my story."

"I am thinking it is all a great miracle," Tabitha answered. "But also a great mystery. How can the Messiah be born to an ordinary woman? I thought he was to come with a mighty army, to destroy our enemy, the Romans."

Zechariah clucked in disgust. "Have you not learned the Torah, child?"

Tabitha thought that was funny, but tried to keep the humor out of her voice. "I'm a girl," she answered. "Girls aren't *allowed* to learn the Torah."

"Oh, uh, yes," Zachariah mumbled. "Of course." Then, after a moment, he added, "I think that is a silly rule!"

Tabitha grinned. "You think girls should be taught as the boys are?" she asked.

"Why not?" the old priest answered. "I have yet to see a girl who cannot outthink a boy at most things!"

Tabitha decided Zechariah would be her new best friend, right after Bartholomew and

97

Jotham. Out loud she said, "It is nice to hear someone say that. Even my father does not believe as you do."

"Be gentle with your father," Zechariah said. "Children usually do not know what their parents really think or believe on such matters."

Tabitha thought about this for a few moments, then said, "Now, what about the Messiah?"

"Oh, yes," Zechariah answered. "Well, let's see, where to start . . . hmm, I suppose the best place is with the prophets . . ."

And with that, Zechariah began a long explanation that lasted through the ups and downs of two whole canyons. He explained how the prophets of old had told of the birth of the Messiah, that it would be to an unmarried woman, and that it would happen in a town called Bethlehem. He told how the entire life of the Messiah had already been explained in Scripture, long before he was born, because it was something God had planned, not man. And when Zechariah had finished this second story, Tabitha was even more amazed than after the first.

"So why don't we go to Bethlehem?" Tabitha asked. "We could be there to see the birth of the Messiah!"

"And what of your father?" Zechariah asked. "Shall we leave him in the hands of the Romans?"

Tabitha's heart fell. "No, of course not. But couldn't we go there after we rescue him?"

Zechariah didn't answer, so Tabitha looked up. She saw the old priest standing still at the top of the next ridge, looking intently at the valley below. The way he stared, Tabitha knew there was something wrong. "What is it?" she asked as she reached the top of the hill herself. "What do you see?"

Zechariah pointed to a plain far below. "A caravan," he said, and Tabitha strained to see where he pointed. "And there is trouble about."

Tabitha couldn't figure out how he knew there was trouble when she couldn't even see the caravan itself, but she kept quiet.

"Come," Zechariah said abruptly, starting down the hill. "We must aid them."

"Aid who?" Tabitha cried, running after him. "How do you know they need help? And how do you know it is not Decha of Megiddo?"

"Decha?" Zechariah asked. "How could it be . . . look, child! Do you not see the colorful tents and handsome animals? This is not the caravan of thieves, but of rich traders! Persians, I'd guess. And I know there is trouble because the caravan is stopped in the middle of the desert, and its people are running about in the hills!"

Tabitha could not see any of this, but believed that he saw what he said. He was proven right a short time later when they reached the bottom of the hill and walked out onto the plain. The tents were truly beautiful, Tabitha could see now, and billowed in the sun like a field of flowers. Zechariah spotted a dark-skinned man just heading into the rocks and called to him.

"Oy there!" Zechariah sang out. "What is your trouble, and could you use some more eyes?"

The man jumped at the sound of Zechariah's voice, but then climbed down from the rock and rushed over to them.

"We search for two lost boys," he said, huffing. "And we could indeed use more eyes!"

Zechariah held out his hand. "I am Zechariah, priest of the temple of Jehovah," he said.

The other man grasped Zechariah's forearm and said, "I am Salamar, astrologer for the Sheik Konarak. I would be honored to have your help."

"How is it the boys are missing?" Zechariah asked. "And what are their names?"

"The boys went off playing while the caravan slept," Salamar answered. "One is my son, Ishtar. The other his friend and my ward, by the name of Jotham."

"Jotham!" Tabitha screeched. "Jotham is *here*?!"

Salamar looked at the girl who had interrupted. "No," he said shortly, "he is *not* here. That is the problem."

"How may we help?" Zechariah asked, and soon the two travelers found themselves hiking through the hills, calling out the names of the two boys. Mid-afternoon, they all met back at Salamar's tent.

"I fear we must leave you now," Zechariah said. "We have seen no sign of the boys, and I must get this young girl to Jerusalem. The Romans have taken a disliking to her father, and we must fetch him an important document."

"Very well," Salamar sighed. "I thank you for your help. I wish I could know where . . ."

Before he could finish his sentence, Salamar was interrupted by a runner from the hills. "We . . . we found some marks on the ground," the man huffed. "Ishtar and the other boy . . . they entered a cave. And right behind them," he added between breaths, "right behind them were the tracks of three men!"

"Decha!" Zechariah spat out the name.

"Who?" Salamar asked.

"Decha of Megiddo. He is a thief, a villain, and a murderer!"

Salamar's dark skin went pale. "Form a brigade!" he yelled to his men. "We go to the cave to search for my son!"

"And Jotham!" Tabitha cried.

"And Jotham!" Salamar added.

Ten of Salamar's men raced into the hills to search for the missing boys. As they did, Tabitha had a terrible feeling they would not find them.

Long before Jesus was born, God told the story of his birth to the people of Israel. He told the story so that they—and we—would have no doubt that Jesus is God's Son.

> Therefore the Lord himself will give you a sign: The virgin will be with child and will give birth to a son, and will call him Immanuel.
>
> ISAIAH 7:14

God wanted us to know that he is in control of history—past, present, and future. *He* decided when the Messiah would come, *he* decided how it would happen, *he* decided where the birth would take place:

> "But you, Bethlehem Ephrathah, though you are small among the clans of Judah, out of you will come for me one who will be ruler over Israel, whose origins are from of old, from ancient times."
>
> MICAH 5:2

So the prophecies of Jesus' birth tell us at least two things: Jesus really is the Son of God, and God has the world safely under control.

Do those thoughts comfort you?

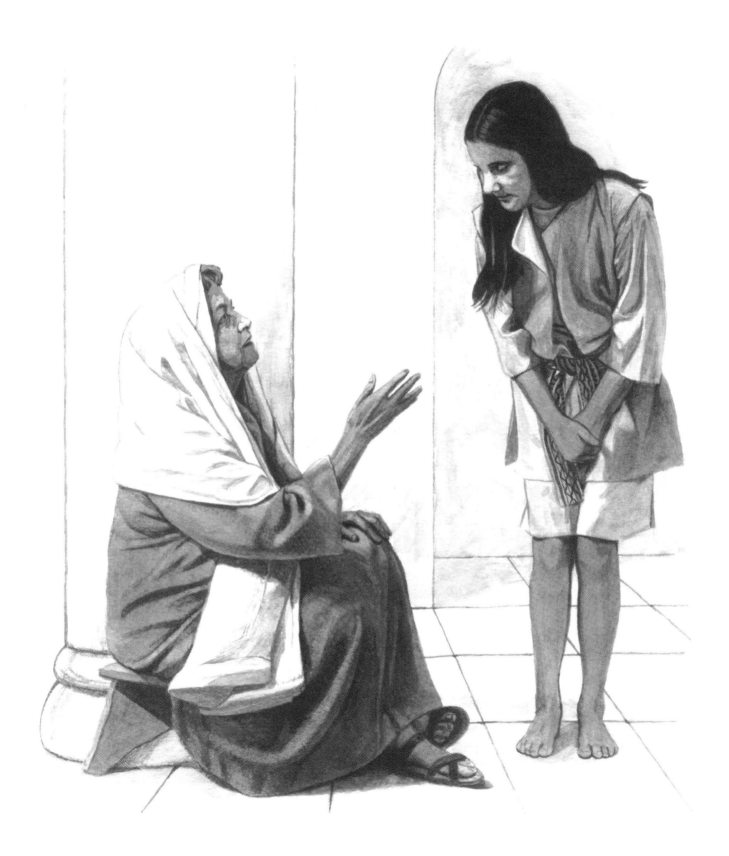

The Temple

Light two violet candles and the pink candle.

W e must take our leave now," Zechariah said to Salamar, their host. "We must reach Jerusalem soon, if we are to save Tabitha's father."

"And we must remain here until the boys are found," Salamar said. "We each have our destinies, and the stars . . . or your God . . . will guide us."

"Selah!" answered Zechariah in the way of the priests. Salamar ordered that food and water for the trip be brought to the travelers. "Rahjahn!" he called to one of his servants. "Take our fastest camel and ride back to Qumran. Tell the monk Nathan that Jotham is once again lost." Turning back to Zechariah he said, "My friend has a right to know that the ward he entrusted to me is missing."

Zechariah nodded, then said to Tabitha, "We must depart now. It is not far to Jerusalem, but the road is rough." Tabitha looked across the sharp volcanic rocks and nodded. "Many blessings on you and your son," she said to Salamar. "May you find him and Jotham being well cared for!"

Salamar seemed surprised that a girl could offer such a blessing. "You remind me of my wife," he said with a smile, and Tabitha took that to be a good thing.

With a wave goodbye, Tabitha and Zechariah once again set out toward Jerusalem. *He was right*, thought Tabitha of the old priest. *This road* is *rough!* In places it seemed as if the trail were nothing more than piles of sharp stones!

"You have fine walking legs," Zechariah said, and Tabitha smiled happily at the compliment. Then he added, "For a girl," and her smile abruptly turned into a glare. She knew better than to speak disrespectfully to an elder, but that didn't keep the harsh words from spinning around inside her head. After a few moments, her guardian turned and looked back at her. "You are quiet," he said. "Have you no thanks for a compliment?"

Tabitha stewed for a moment, trying not to let anything sarcastic out of her mouth. "I thank you for the compliment," she said finally. "But I would rather be complimented as a person, not just as a girl."

"Ahh, I see," said the old man, turning back to the trail before him. "So you think it a disdainful thing to be a girl?"

"No!" Tabitha almost shouted. "I do not disdain being a girl! But I disdain the way girls are treated."

Zechariah was quiet for a moment, then said, "I, too, think it is wrong the way women are treated. That is one reason my wife and I live so far from the city. She is my companion in every way, and my equal in most. But," he continued, "it is not the way of our people. And we must each humble ourselves to the place which God has appointed us. You must humble yourself to your parents and your elders, I must humble myself to the service of God, my wife, and you."

"Me!" Tabitha said, unable to believe what she was hearing. "You are a servant to me?"

Zechariah stopped and looked back at her again. "Do I not serve you now," he asked, "by taking you to find your father? Did I not leave my home and my wife and my work in order to be of service to you?"

Tabitha's mouth hung open for a moment, then she slowly nodded her head in agreement.

"Well then," Zechariah said as he continued walking, "if a priest of God can humble himself to the service of a child, perhaps that child could humble herself to the service of others as well. Even if they are boys! I do not think you should be treated as less important because you are a girl, Tabitha. But I do think you should treat others as more important than yourself, because you are a child of the most holy God."

Tabitha had to think on these things for a long while, and by the time her old thoughts had made room for these new ones, she and Zechariah had reached the top of a hill overlooking a magnificent city.

"And so we greet Jerusalem," Zechariah announced.

Jerusalem! So many buildings, so many people and animals, and so much noise it could be heard even from this hilltop. But what caught Tabitha's eye first was the temple that soared into the air like a mountain of white granite. The city was built on another, lower hilltop, and capped it off like a crown of jewels. A green valley cut by a blue stream separated the two travelers from the city, but would easily be forded.

"What do you think?" Zechariah asked at last.

"I think it is the most magnificent thing I have ever seen!" Tabitha gasped. "Can we go there now?"

The old priest laughed. "Yes, oh anxious one, we can go there now." And in less time than it takes to pluck a chicken, they had hiked down the hill, crossed the valley and the stream, and entered a gate in the wall of the city. Had she not known differently, Tabitha might have thought this Hebron, so similar were the narrow streets. But it was obviously not En Gedi, for the people here were much more reserved. And it was not Jericho, because there was none of the vast open spaces of that city. It was crowded, and stuffy, and smelly—and Tabitha loved it!

"Where shall we look first?" Tabitha asked.

"At the temple," Zechariah answered. "I must inform my elders of my presence, and will ask them for any news of your father."

Tabitha was thrilled at the thought of entering the temple. They pushed their way through the crowds until they came to a long climb of pure white, marble steps. The steps led to a wall where guards stood watch at a gate. The guards eyed Zechariah carefully, then nodded to him, allowing him in. Tabitha followed. Inside the wall was a courtyard full of vendors. They were sellers of doves and incense and many things Tabitha did not recognize.

"Why do these people sell here?" she whispered. "Is this not the house of God?"

"Yes, of course," Zechariah answered. "They sell the birds and animals people need to offer sacrifices for their sins."

Tabitha nodded understanding, and followed Zechariah through a doorway in another wall to another courtyard. Here women sat by themselves praying, or stood in small groups talking quietly. *This is a much more pleasant place*, Tabitha thought. Zechariah reached a door in yet another wall, and stopped.

"You may not accompany me any farther," he said. "This door leads to the court of men."

Tabitha's face began to warm in anger, but then she remembered Zechariah's words on the trail and forced the feelings back down to her toes. "Then I shall humble myself to God's service," she said, "and wait for you with the women."

Zechariah smiled. "It is difficult, I know," he said. "But it will not always be so." Then he went through the door and was gone. Tabitha wasn't sure if he meant that it would not always be difficult, or that women would not always be treated such, but either way she took comfort in his words and began wandering around the courtyard.

Suddenly there was a sharp yank on Tabitha's tunic. "Girl!" she heard an old, squeaky voice say. "Girl!" the voice said again, with two more tugs on her tunic. Tabitha looked down to see an ancient woman seated at the base of a column. The woman was dressed in rags, but was as clean as if she had just been washed in Noah's flood.

"Yes, Mother?" Tabitha answered in the polite way of her people.

"Girl!" the woman said again. "The Messiah is coming!"

Tabitha gasped and knelt down. "Yes! This I have heard! Do you know when?"

The woman was surprised by Tabitha's reaction. But she looked her in the eyes and whispered, "Within the week, this miracle shall happen."

Tabitha blinked a few times. "Less than a week!"

"Yes, and even sooner!" Then she asked, "What are you doing here alone? Where is your mother?"

A dove building a nest atop a nearby column made seven complete trips for twigs in the time it took Tabitha to tell the old woman her story.

"Jotham of Jericho, you say?" the woman said, filing the name away in her head. "I shall watch for him. And what of your father? How would I know him?"

"He is a tall man, a shepherd. He is a Jew, but also a citizen of Rome, though the Romans won't believe him."

The old woman looked up in surprise. "I know of this man!" she said. "And I know where they have taken him!"

Tabitha is finding it difficult to submit herself to others, especially when she doesn't agree with their viewpoints.

"Submit" is one of the toughest words in the New Testament for us to accept, and about the toughest to do. It means giving up our rights—giving up our wills—to people with whom we may not even agree.

And yet, that's exactly what God has told us we must do.

Jesus submitted to the will of his Father in coming to earth, living a godly life, and dying a sacrificial death at the hands of people who wrongly accused him. He submitted to earthly authorities as well, even though he knew those authorities to be evil. So is it too much for God to ask that we submit to those in authority over us?

God gives us the freedom of choice to do as we please, then asks us to freely choose to give up that freedom! At first that may not seem to make sense, but it's really for our own good: there's only room in our lives for one God. We either have to let God be God, or take on that job ourselves. Submitting to those in authority over us—humbling ourselves before man and God—is how we show God that we honor and respect him as Lord of our lives.

> Clothe yourselves with humility toward one another, because, "God opposes
> the proud but gives grace to the humble."   1 PETER 5:5

Antonia

Light two violet candles and the pink candle.

What news do you have of my father?" Tabitha gasped.

The old woman closed her eyes, raised her face to the sun, then began to speak. "They brought the man here in chains," she whispered. "A tall man, a shepherd and a Jew, and two others with him. They mocked him, calling him 'citizen,' bowing down to him as insult. Then they took him to the Fortress of Antonia, on the other side of the city, where he sits even now in a dungeon cell waiting to be executed."

Tears came to Tabitha's eyes as the old woman finished. She was about to ask how the woman knew all this when Zechariah's voice thundered from behind her. "Tabitha!" he barked. "We must go!"

Tabitha looked back at the priest, then at the woman, who was now staring at her. "I thank you for this information," Tabitha said. "And what may I call you?"

"I am Anna," the woman said, "daughter of Phanuel, and a prophetess of God!"

"Tabitha! Come!" Zechariah shouted.

"I must go now," Tabitha said to Anna. "We must save my father, and then go to Bethlehem to see the Messiah!"

"I shall send Jotham of Jericho your way, should our paths meet."

Tabitha stood and ran over to Zechariah who said, "I have had no fortune in finding information on your father," he said.

"I have!" Tabitha said, to the old priest's surprise. "He is a prisoner in the Fortress of Antonia!"

"Antonia!" Zechariah gasped. "That is the fortress built by Herod, but now used by the Roman Legion. We must go there at once!"

As they headed back out through the court of women, and then the court of the gentiles, Tabitha considered that, if she had not been stopped from following Zechariah into the temple, she would never have met Anna. *Perhaps God knows what he's doing after all*, she decided.

Zechariah led the way out through the front gate and down the many stairs of marble. He turned to the right, into the very heart of Jerusalem, dragging Tabitha behind him by the hand. Turning first one way and then the other down the streets, he led them in such a maze that Tabitha knew she would never find her way out by herself. As they approached a street wider than the rest, they began to hear the shouts of a great crowd of people. Making one last turn, Tabitha saw a mob of people, all of them looking away from her, toward the end of the street. She looked up too, and saw there a tall tower, surrounded by a wall protected by Roman soldiers.

"The Fortress of Antonia?" she asked.

"Yes," Zechariah answered. "And trouble brewing as well."

A moment later screams erupted from the other end of the street. The crowd parted like the Red Sea, and Tabitha watched as a dozen men—Jews, by the look of them—came running up the street with swords in their hands. They ran past Tabitha so close that she could smell the sweat on their bodies, and see the terror on their faces. But before she even had time to think about these things, she heard the thunder of running horses. She looked back just in time to see four of the huge animals galloping up the street, each with a Roman soldier on its back. The soldiers kicked their horses to go faster, and in a flash they pounded past Tabitha such that the very ground shook.

As the Jews and the Romans vanished down the street, the crowd of people began milling about, talking about what they had just witnessed. Opinions were flying like dust in a storm, and some even suggested that they all join the Zealots.

"Zealots?" Tabitha questioned. "What is a Zealot?"

Zachariah shook his head in disgust. "They are Jews who do not know how to behave as Jews," he said. "They think that by causing trouble for the Romans, they will free us from tyranny."

"Should we not fight back when we can?" Tabitha asked.

"We should follow the ways of Jehovah," Zechariah answered, "even when it does not make sense to us."

Tabitha thought about that for a moment, and thought it made a lot of sense.

"Come now," the priest said, "let us see what has taken place at Antonia."

They pushed their way down the street as people continued to gossip about the Zealots. From what they said, Tabitha learned that the Zealots had tried to attack the fortress, but had been easily beaten back by the Romans. Inside, she shivered at the thought that the attack might cause more problems for her father.

Finally the two travelers reached the base of the fortress. It was made of red stone, and had a long stairway up to the gate, much like at the temple. A ring of soldiers stood guard around the base of the stairway. They held their spears out at arm's length, with the wooden end braced against the ground. This allowed the sun to glint off the spears, drawing Tabitha's attention to their deadly, pointed tips.

"Hold!" one of the soldiers barked at Zechariah. "Do not approach, or you will die!"

The priest bowed and said, "I am no Zealot, and no threat. I seek only information on a prisoner."

"There is no information here that a Jew needs, except that he will die if he defies Rome!"

"I know this well," Zechariah said. "But the information is not for me, it is for this poor child here."

"A Jew is a Jew," the Roman sneered. "Now stand away!"

All the time Zechariah was talking to one Roman soldier, Tabitha was watching another. He was behind the line of standing soldiers, but was lying on the ground, bleeding. Without asking and without even thinking, she pushed her way between two of the guards and ran to the injured man. Instantly she saw that he was wounded in the side. She ripped off the arm of her tunic and held the cloth on the wound.

Meanwhile, the soldier closest to Zechariah whipped around and raised his spear. He pulled back his arm and was ready to release his weapon when Zechariah grabbed the end of the spear and knocked it to the ground. Furious, the soldier spun around and snatched up the spear, this time aiming it at the priest.

"Hold!"

The voice sounded like the roar of an angry lion, and instantly got the attention of all the guards. The soldier about to skewer Zechariah turned toward the voice and yelled, "Hold? But Centurion, this Jew attacked me!"

"I saw many Zealots attack today," the voice continued. "This priest was not among them. And why would you kill a small girl whose only crime is helping one of your comrades?"

Tabitha finally found the source of the voice: a tall, broad Roman. Gold ornaments glittered on his red cape. He stood firmly at the top of the stairs, his fists on his hips, eyeing the soldier who threatened Zechariah.

"Lower your lance," the centurion commanded. Then, with hands still on his hips, he walked the dozen steps down to where Tabitha tended the wounded man.

"Will he live?" the centurion asked.

"I believe so," Tabitha answered. "The wound is shallow, and I have stopped the bleeding."

The centurion nodded, then lowered himself on one knee, putting his face close to Tabitha's. "Why would a Jewish girl help a Roman soldier?" he asked.

Tabitha didn't hesitate to answer. "Because he is in need of help," she said.

The centurion stared at her for a long time, then nodded. "And what is a Jewish girl doing at the Fortress of Antonia in the first place?"

Tabitha gulped, then looked at Zechariah on the street below. Zechariah nodded, urging her to tell the Roman the truth, and so she did.

When she had finished, the centurion stared at her for another long time.

"I know of this case," he said. "And I know the fate of your father."

Jesus said, "Love your enemies and pray for those who persecute you" (Matthew 5:44).

What a strange idea! *Love* those who *hate* us? Why would he say such a thing?

Probably because he has seen the power of hate, and the power of love, and knows which one works. "God is love," 1 John tells us, so much love that there can be no hate or violence in him. So since we are created in God's image, shouldn't we reflect that love toward others?

It's easy to be angry, easy to hate. It's very difficult to love as Christ did. Tabitha is filled with natural love and compassion for people that allow her to care even for her enemies. As the day approaches when we will celebrate Christ's birth, are there any "enemies" that *you* need to start loving?

Vanished

Light two violet candles and the pink candle.

Tabitha stared into the eyes of the Roman centurion, afraid to hear the words he might speak. She saw that they were cold eyes, the eyes of a man familiar with killing. But she also saw the smallest touch of compassion. It was this compassion that finally prompted her to ask the question, "What of my father?"

The Roman's expression did not change, but when he spoke it was in a low voice, as if he didn't want his soldiers to hear. "He was held here these last several days," he said, "and was to be executed this very morning. But his claim of being a citizen worried my commander, so he sent your father to Herodium, to be judged by a Roman officer named Coponius."

Tabitha's heart leapt at the news that her father was still alive. Then she saw the Roman's forehead wrinkle, as if worried. He looked about to make sure no one could hear, then said, "Emperor Augustus has heard rumors that King Herod has become insane, and sent Coponius here to investigate. Since he was sent by Rome, Coponius will judge your father, and he will judge him fairly. But you must hurry," the centurion added. "If you have proof of his citizenship, you must get it to Herodium by morning, or your father will be executed."

Now Tabitha's heart sank, wondering how in all of Palestine she would do such a thing. Suddenly the Roman stood to his feet. "Release the priest!" he commanded, "and let these two go their way!"

The soldiers surrounding Zechariah stepped back into line. A physician had arrived by now and was tending to the wounded man. "A fine job you did stopping the bleeding," he said to Tabitha. "You will make a good midwife."

"Hurry now," the centurion said. Then he leaned down and whispered in her ear, "And remember from this day, that not all Romans are evil!"

Tabitha smiled at the soldier, but he did not smile back. He must not show any weakness to his men, she decided. Then she ran down the steps, grabbed Zechariah by the hand, and yelled, "Come on!"

Running up the street the old priest yelled to her, "Where are we going?"

"To Herodium," Tabitha answered.

Zechariah skidded to a stop, with Tabitha still tugging on his hand. "Why are you stopping?" she cried, pulling now with both hands. "We must hurry!"

"Because child," Zechariah said patiently, "you are going the wrong way."

An hour later, Tabitha and her priest-protector were on the south road, out of Jerusalem. After listening to Tabitha's report of the centurion's words, Zechariah had enlisted the help of Obadiah, one of his priest friends, sending the man to Bethlehem to fetch the needed parchment. He and Tabitha would head straight to Herodium. Perhaps the plea of a daughter would stay the executioner's hand long enough for Obadiah to bring the evidence.

"How far is it?" Tabitha asked.

"The sun will just be setting when we arrive," Zechariah answered. Then he added, "It is not far."

They continued walking at a quick pace, passing many other travelers along the way. The sun was headed down, and Tabitha thought they must be getting close. Suddenly, Zechariah let out a squeal and began hopping on one foot. "What is it?" Tabitha asked. "A scorpion?"

"No, no such trouble," Zechariah said. He sat on a rock and pulled his injured foot up on his knee. "Just a thorn," he said. He pulled the sticker from his foot and winced, then began rubbing his troubled sole. "I must rest a short while," he said. "Then we will continue."

Tabitha was frustrated at the delay, but said nothing except, "I shall search this hillside for some berries while you rest."

As Zechariah continued rubbing his foot, Tabitha climbed the hill behind him, taking in the view. Off in the distance, another hour's walk by her judgment, she saw a palace on a hill. That must be Herodium, she thought. *How beautiful!* She continued gazing at the sight until, from the other side of the hill, she heard a soft cry. Leaving Herodium behind, she crested the hill to see a man, a woman, and a donkey in a small hollow. The woman was on the ground, and appeared to be pregnant and in pain.

"May I be of help?" Tabitha cried as she ran down to the couple.

The man looked up. "My wife is soon to give birth," he said, "and is weary from travel."

Tabitha stared at the woman, and thought she looked a lot like an angel must look. She was breathing quickly, and her lips were cracked and dry. "Would you care for a sip of water?" Tabitha asked.

"That is most kind," the woman answered. "Our skin of water ran out earlier this afternoon, and there have been no more streams or wells."

Without a word, Tabitha pulled her own water skin out of her travel bag. She handed it to the man, who helped his wife take a long drink. When she was finished, the woman looked much cooler and breathed more comfortably.

"Your kindness speaks well of your father," the woman said.

At the word "father" Tabitha suddenly remembered her quest. "Forgive me," she sputtered, "but I must leave you now. Is there any other need you have?"

"No, thank you, child," the man said. "Your kindness has been a great help already."

Tabitha ran back up the hill, then down the other side to where Zechariah was standing. "I thought you had gone on without me!" he said.

"Forgive me," Tabitha replied as they began walking again. "I found a woman in need, and shared my water with her."

Zechariah shook his head in wonder. "I believe you could find a way to help Decha himself!"

Tabitha just shrugged. "Perhaps Jehovah has found a job for my life," she said.

A short time later they turned a bend in the road and found themselves at the foot of the hill on which rested the palace of Herodium. Tabitha gawked as she looked straight up, wondering how anyone could build such a towering fortress on top of a hill.

"And a man-made hill at that," Zechariah said when she voiced her wonder. "Ten thousand slaves worked seven years to build this mountain, so that Herod could have his palace."

The thought of Jews being enslaved for such work sickened Tabitha, and suddenly the palace didn't look quite so beautiful.

At the base of the hill of Herodium sat the town of Herodium, and it was here that Zechariah and Tabitha finally found some dinner at an inn. As she devoured the pasty mixture of fish and oats, Tabitha asked her guardian, "Why do men make slaves of other men?"

Zechariah looked up from his own bowl and stared for a moment. "Because they do not understand that there can be only one God over men. They think it is important to be gods themselves."

"Why does Jehovah allow such things to happen?"

"He cannot stop us if we are to have the choice to be good or evil," Zechariah said, taking a bite of bread. "All he can promise is to use even the worst of situations for our good."

Tabitha nodded, then scooped up the last dollop of paste. "May I have more?" she asked.

Zechariah laughed. "You certainly have the appetite of a boy!" he said. He took her bowl, got up from the table, and worked his way through the crowded inn to the cooking area. He handed the innkeeper a small coin, and in return received another bowl of the gruel. Holding the bowl up high so as not to spill it, he worked his way back to the table. But then he stopped dead in his tracks.

Tabitha was gone.

For I was hungry and you gave me something to eat, I was thirsty and you gave me something to drink, I was a stranger and you invited me in.

MATTHEW 25:35

Compassionate is a word often used to describe Jesus. We could probably use it to describe the character of Tabitha as well. Is it a word others would use to describe you?

Being compassionate toward others—helping others in need—is part of what it means to love. It doesn't call on us to judge them for their situation. It doesn't give us the choice to care only for the people we like. It's not something we can do only when it's convenient for us. It is a command, part of the command Jesus gave to "love your neighbor as yourself."

To be compassionate means much more than to feel sorry for someone. It means having a strong desire—and acting on that desire—to help them, even at the expense of our own comfort.

"I tell you the truth," Jesus said, "whatever you did for one of the least of these brothers of mine, you did for me." When we give a sip of water to one of God's children who is thirsty, it's as if we are giving it to Jesus himself.

Imagine that!

Kidnapped

Light two violet candles and the pink candle.

Tabitha pulled at the bindings around her wrists, but with her arms tied tightly behind her back, she could not break loose. The cloth tied in her mouth like the bit on a horse kept her screams from being heard. But nothing could keep the stench of dead animals from her nose.

She had been sitting at the table in the inn, thinking about her father, when a rough and smelly hand covered her face. Arms as thick as a camel's thigh lifted her off her stool and clamped tightly around her waist. Tabitha screamed, of course, but as her abductor slipped through the crowd of traders, travelers, and taxpayers, they all just turned and looked the other way. Before she could say *dancing camels*, she had been carried to the back room of a butcher shop. Blood covered the walls and floors from the hundreds of animals slaughtered here. It made everything black, and sticky, with a horrible smell.

Tabitha struggled again, trying to loosen the bindings on her wrists or ankles. *If only I could stretch them a bit*, she thought. But the cloth was well broken in, and any stretch it once had was pulled from it long ago. The thought that she should be crying passed through Tabitha's head, but she quickly decided that if she were going to free herself and save her father, she didn't have time for such things. *Crying is something Rachel would do*, she thought. *I must be stronger than that.*

And yet, no matter how hard she thought or how much she struggled, she could find no way out of the situation. The walls were strong, and she had heard the locking bolt on the other side of the door slide into place when her captor had left her here.

The room was empty, at least as far as she could see, except for a heavy, square table in the middle, and half of a deer hanging from the ceiling. But it was dark, with only a few cracks of light coming through the boards of the door. Tabitha began to shiver, fearing what might happen to her, and where she would be taken. "Jehovah, help me!" she whispered over and over.

The bolt slammed open with a "crack!" and Tabitha jumped. Her heart began to race as the door swung inward. A man stood in the doorway, but he was lit from the back so she couldn't see his face. He stood a moment, then walked over to Tabitha. Now she could see that it was not the same man who had kidnapped her; this one was smaller and more round. The man leaned down and looked her over closely.

"Yes, you will do nicely," the man said. He had an accent that Tabitha did not recognize, and he dressed in the strange clothes of some other world. "You'll fetch a good price," he continued, "and then you'll be off to Rome where you'll have a pleasant life as slave girl to a master."

The man did not speak with a cruel voice. In fact, Tabitha thought, he sounded no more concerned than if he were telling her he should go home to feed his dog. This was a business deal, Tabitha realized. *He's a seller, and I'm his wares!* This made her furious, and she began kicking at the man. But he only stood and stepped back.

"You should save your strength," he said, looking down on her. "The voyage to Rome will not be as pleasant as this room."

The thought that any place could be worse than this slaughterhouse made Tabitha gag. She must do everything possible to try to escape. She must save her father!

The man turned and headed back to the door. In that instant Tabitha wormed her way to her feet, ran across the room and threw herself at the man's back. He spun around, surprised, and she butted him in the stomach with her head like a goat. At that moment the outer door of the butcher shop opened, and Tabitha saw a woman enter. In that split second, the woman saw Tabitha, or so it seemed to the captive girl, but then the man pushed her down with his foot and slammed the door shut.

As fast as she could, Tabitha scooted over to the door and found a crack wide enough that she could see through.

"I have come for some deer meat," the muffled voice of the woman said. "I heard you have some fresh. I will require the hindquarter."

"The shop is closed," a man's voice said gruffly, and Tabitha supposed it must be her original captor. "Come back tomorrow."

"I am not here for myself," the woman said, and it seemed to Tabitha that she must be a very bold woman to talk that way to a man. "I am the new cook for King Herod, and he awaits me in the fortress."

Tabitha didn't need to see the man's face to know he had turned pale. "For . . . forgive me, good lady!" he stammered. "I will personally deliver the meat to the fortress within the hour!"

"Very well," the woman answered coldly. "If I am pleased, you will have more business from me in the future."

Tabitha couldn't believe that a woman could have such power over a man, and couldn't let this opportunity for rescue pass. As the woman was speaking, Tabitha began kicking at the door and screaming through the gag in her mouth. After a few moments she stopped to hear what effect her cry for help may have had. The butcher was obviously frightened.

"Ignore the racket," he told the woman, trying to usher her out the door. "It is just a goat who does not look forward to being butchered."

"Or perhaps a young girl you have kidnapped to sell into slavery!" the woman said tartly.

Tabitha could see the butcher's face now as well. *Surely this powerful woman will save me*, she thought.

"Good lady, there is no girl—"

The woman silenced him with an upheld hand. "There is a girl," she said. "But fear not, your business is your own. I came only for meat, not intrigue."

The butcher relaxed, and promised the cook excellent meat at a fair price as he finally got her out the door. Once it had closed behind her, the butcher seemed to collapse into a mound of jelly. "We must move the girl soon," he said. Tabitha realized the other man must still be in the shop.

"Yes," the other voice said. "But first you must deliver your goods as promised. She will surely tell the guards what she has seen if you are late."

"Agreed," was all the first man said. A moment later the door to Tabitha's jail cell opened and the butcher walked in. He carried a large cleaver in his hand, and stopped to look down on Tabitha. "I should use this on you," he said, "for making all that noise." He began hacking away at the deer carcass as he continued. "But all is well, and you will fetch a good price if you are alive, and none at all if you are dead."

A few minutes later, the butcher hefted the hindquarter of deer over his shoulder and left the room. The door slammed shut, and Tabitha heard the bolt slide into place once more. Several minutes passed as Tabitha heard the man working on the meat. After a while, the butcher left to deliver the venison to the palace.

It was then that Tabitha realized she had stopped shivering. In fact, she wasn't afraid at all. It was as if Jehovah were sitting right there next to her, his arm around her, promising to care for her.

A few minutes later the butcher returned. "What about the girl?" he asked.

There was a pause, then the other man said, "Go get her."

Once again, Tabitha finds herself in a terrifying situation. Once again, she calls on God for help. Once again, he hears her and answers. Do *you* have that kind of faith?

Being friends with Jesus isn't just a mental exercise—it's not just something we do in our heads. He is real, he is alive, and our friendship with him is real and alive. But it's not something we can stick in a drawer until we're in trouble. Like any other friendship, we have to keep working at it. We have to talk to Jesus every day, tell him how we feel about what's happening in our lives, tell him we love him. Then, when the tough times come, he's already right there next to us, waiting to help us, like any good friend.

> The LORD is close to the brokenhearted and saves those who are crushed in spirit.
> PSALM 34:18

When we celebrate Christmas, we are celebrating that the God who created the universe has chosen to come down and live among us, and in us. Develop that friendship; get to know Jesus. He's here to help whenever you need it. All you have to do is ask.

Dark Figures

Light two violet candles and the pink candle.

Tabitha sucked in her breath and held it. Her heart began to race and sweat popped out on her neck. The door slammed open and the bright light slapped her in the face. Squinting at the shadowy figure of the butcher, she scooted back into the corner, trying to get away. But his powerful arms lifted her easily, and the man carried her to the other room and dumped her in a chair.

The second man looked her over again, holding a lamp up next to her face. He forced her lips apart, then squeezed her arm. "Huh, good, strong arms," he said. "Clean her up and we'll take her to Gaius."

Tabitha had no idea who Gaius was, but the one thing she did know made her shiver in fright: the name Gaius was a Roman name.

The butcher dipped a cloth in water and scrubbed Tabitha's face so hard that it stung. She glared at the man, but had determined she would say nothing; she would not amuse them by crying or pleading. Then he ran a comb through her hair and brushed off her clothing. "That will have to do," he said when he had finished. The second man eyed Tabitha again.

"Well, she should fetch at least a hundred shekels," he said. Then he added, "Too bad she's not a boy. They're worth so much more."

Tabitha sat up straight like a snake ready to strike and glared at the man, her lips pursed tightly.

"Do not be offended," the man said without humor. "It is not your fault that boys are worth more than girls." Then, as if he had some measure of compassion for the girl, he leaned close and said, "You will like being a slave to Gaius. He'll treat you kindly, and allow you much freedom once you've earned it. And," he added, "you will get to see Rome. Isn't that a wondrous thought?"

Tabitha's thoughts spun around in her head like a windstorm. *Rome! I don't want to go to Rome. And I don't want to be a slave, no matter how kind the master! I want to save my father! I want to go home!*

The man stood back and motioned to the butcher. "Time to go," he said, and lifted her from the chair. As he did so, Tabitha was able to see out the window, and there was a most glorious sight: the priest Zechariah, walking straight toward the butcher shop! Instantly Tabitha began to kick and squirm, and let out a muffled yell through her gag. The butcher held her tightly and said, "Stop fighting me, girl, or it will only be worse for you!"

But then the other man looked out the window and saw Zechariah. "Quickly!" he hissed. "Take her into the slaughterhouse!"

Now the butcher looked up and saw the priest approaching. Silently he dragged Tabitha back into the smelly room, and took her to the far corner. He threw her on the ground, then fell on top of her. Between the weight of the butcher and the gag in her mouth, Tabitha had to gasp to get even a little air to breathe. The butcher weighed as much as a cow, and she could almost feel her bones snapping in two.

Tabitha heard the outer door open and Zechariah's muffled voice talking with the other man. The conversation lasted several minutes, during which Tabitha struggled to get the butcher off of her, or to make some sound that would alert the priest.

"Perhaps she got lost in your storeroom," Tabitha heard Zechariah say. They were the first words she heard clearly, and she realized he had moved close to the door. Squirming to her right, she looked up and saw his shadow through the cracks between the boards. Then another shadow moved next to the first.

"I'm afraid the only thing lost in our storeroom is a hindquarter of deer meat," she heard him say.

There was a long pause, and Tabitha could imagine the priest searching the face of the other man. "Very well," he said finally. "But if you should happen to see her, please send a message to the inn of Joshua."

There was another pause, and Tabitha strained her hardest to free some part of her body that could kick the wall or slap the floor or make any kind of sound at all. But then the shadows left, and she heard the front door open and close again. A moment later, the door to the storeroom opened.

"He's gone," the man said. "Let's get rid of this girl before she causes us more trouble!"

Tabitha sucked in a deep breath of air as the man finally stopped smothering her. The gag was still stuffed into her mouth, but at least the weight of the cow was off her chest!

The butcher pulled Tabitha up under his arm again, and the three of them headed out the front door. It was well after dark by now, and few people were about. Those who *were* out looked like mangy dogs, Tabitha thought, and couldn't have cared less about a girl being sold into slavery.

Hung from the butcher's arm as she was, Tabitha had to twist her neck around in order to see anything. They seemed to be headed up one of the main streets, but then they turned and went down a narrow alley. This part of town was empty, with all the people locked tightly inside their mud and stone houses. Somewhere up ahead a horse whinnied and for a moment Tabitha thought perhaps it would be the horse of a wealthy shepherd who would help her. But it was far away, and there were no other sounds of rescue.

Cold and afraid, Tabitha began to shiver, and thought she might be sick. With each step the butcher took she bounced some more, and that only made her stomach feel worse. *It will serve him right if I throw up all over his feet!* Tabitha thought.

The two men turned another corner, into a part of town Tabitha thought she wouldn't even want to visit in the daylight. *Surely thieves live here*, she thought. *Thieves, and worse!*

At that moment, two dark figures sprang from the shadows. They were dressed in dark cloaks that covered their faces, and raised long clubs. Screaming like madmen, they rushed at the two men and Tabitha, waving the clubs over their heads. The butcher dropped Tabitha, and she fell in the mud and slop of the street. The attackers went after Tabitha's captors, and began beating them on the head and body. The butcher reached for a knife, but the blow of a club knocked it out of his hand. The other man had a sword, but was no match for the two thieves in black. Beaten and bloody, the butcher and his friend ran back the way they had come.

Unwilling to become someone else's prize, Tabitha scrambled to her feet and turned down an alley. Her legs and hands were still bound though, and she had only hopped a few feet before the attackers were upon her. The taller one grabbed her by the arm and spun her around.

"Tabitha!" the thief shouted. "It's me!" And as the "thief" threw back the hood of his cloak, Tabitha saw the face of her friend Zechariah.

Stunned for a moment, Tabitha could only stare. Then Zechariah removed the gag and the bindings, and she fell into his arms in tears. So relieved was she that she couldn't even talk to thank her savior.

A few minutes later, still snuffling and sniffling, Tabitha looked over at the other man who had rescued her, wondering who it could be. The man slowly pulled back his hood, and Tabitha saw that it wasn't a man at all, but the cook from the palace!

"We must hurry," the woman said. "I know of your father's case, and we have little time!"

At just the right time, Zechariah and the cook stepped in to save Tabitha.

At just the right time, Christ died to save us from our sins.

Once she understood that the two dark figures were there to help her, did Tabitha fight them off? Did she tell them, "Go away, I don't want your help!"? Did she say, "I'd rather do this myself"?

Of course not. That would have been a very foolish thing to do.

When Jesus reaches out to us with nail-scarred hands and offers to save us from our sins, should we send him away? Should we tell him, "Go away, I don't want your help!"? Should we say to him, "I'd rather be my own god"?

That doesn't seem to make much sense either.

Have you invited Jesus to be the Lord of your life? Have you asked him to forgive you of your sins? Have you accepted him as your Savior?

If not, you have an opportunity to accept the best Christmas present you could ever have. And it's a present that comes straight from God:

For God so loved the world that he gave his one and only Son, that whoever believes in him shall not perish but have eternal life.   JOHN 3:16

If you're ready to accept this gift from God it's very simple: just ask. Tell Jesus you're sorry for your sins and ask him to forgive you. Then ask him to be the Lord of your life.

The moment you sincerely pray this simple prayer, Jesus answers. It's instantaneous. You're forgiven of your sins, and you begin a lifetime of friendship with him.

Merry Christmas!

Special Instructions for Week Four

Because Advent always starts on Sunday but Christmas is on a different day each year, Advent can last anywhere from twenty-one to twenty-eight days. Therefore the last week of *Tabitha's Travels* is in seven parts. The following table will help you determine which parts to read each day this week, depending on which day Christmas Eve falls. (See the chart on page 159.)

If Christmas Eve is on Sunday or Monday, you may want to break up the reading by singing a carol or sharing in some other activity between each part.

Instead of devotional thoughts, each part is followed by a question to consider. Use the question or questions of the day as a discussion starter, or consider them seriously in your own heart. Either way, have a wonderful week: Christmas is coming!

If Christmas Eve is on:

Read these parts on:	Sun	Mon	Tues	Wed	Thur	Fri	Sat
Sunday	1–7	1–5	1–3	1–2	1–2	1	1
Monday		6–7	4–5	3–4	3	2	2
Tuesday			6–7	5	4	3	3
Wednesday				6–7	5	4	4
Thursday					6–7	5	5
Friday						6–7	6
Saturday							7

Tabitha's Travels

*Light the violet candles and the pink candle
each day.*

Part One

Tabitha stared in disbelief. The "man" who had saved her was a woman, and a cook! How could she overpower a thief like the butcher?

"You're a woman!" Tabitha gasped.

"Of course I am," the cook said as she pulled the cloak over her head. Zechariah took his off as well, and they hung the two garments on the line from which they had borrowed them. "Listen, Tabitha, just because you're a girl doesn't mean you're not as good as a boy."

"That's what I've been saying!" Tabitha cried.

Zechariah shushed her, and looked around nervously. "Come," he said, "we must leave this place before the rats come out."

"And we must hurry to save your father!" the cook said.

They walked quickly up the side street then, with Zechariah holding tightly to Tabitha's tunic. "But who are you?" Tabitha asked. "And how do you know my name?"

"Forgive me," Zechariah said as they scurried up the street. "I should have introduced you. Tabitha, this is Naomi, a friend I met this very night. She is the head cook for King Herod, and works in the palace." Zechariah pointed to the palace, towering overhead on top of the hill.

"I saw you when you came to the butcher shop," Tabitha said.

"Yes, and I saw you," Naomi answered. "But I had to pretend I was uninterested. I am not afraid of any man, but could not have rescued you from two."

The three turned onto the main street that ran toward the base of the hill. "So how did you find Zechariah?" Tabitha asked.

"After I left the butcher shop, I hid in the shadows to wait for Jehovah to provide a way to help you. After Zechariah left the shop, I pulled him aside, and together we made this plan. I knew those men would try to sell you to a Roman named Gaius. He's in town looking for slaves."

"Yes!" Tabitha shouted. "That is the name I heard!"

"So we borrowed the cloaks to hide our identities," Zechariah picked up the story, "and used surprise to our favor in rescuing you."

Tabitha turned to Naomi and asked, "What of my father?"

"He is well," Naomi said, "but he won't be for long. He is to go before Herod and Coponius this very night, following the feast being prepared even now."

"Then we truly must hurry!" Tabitha said, but then she stopped with a gasp and looked at Zechariah. "The scrolls!" she cried. "Your servant has not yet returned with my father's proof of citizenship!"

"Fear not, child," Zechariah said. "I shall wait here and bring it the moment he arrives."

"But what if he doesn't?" Tabitha asked.

Zechariah dropped to one knee and looked Tabitha in the eyes. "You must trust in God," he said. "There are many things in this life that we cannot control. You must have faith that God will take care of you *and* your father, either in this life, or in the next."

Tabitha nodded slowly, although she still felt fear. "I will try," she said.

"Come now," Naomi said, pulling Tabitha along. "You will pose as one of my child servants. But pray that we are not caught, or it will be death for both of us."

Tabitha shuddered a little as they headed up the steep road to the palace. She looked back to see Zechariah waving goodbye, and decided to believe that Jehovah really was still with her.

At the top of the hill, Naomi led Tabitha around the side of the walled fortress. Tabitha gawked at the gold and marble pillars of the main entrance as they went by, but knew they would have to use the servants' entrance. As they walked along a narrow trail, a Jewish guard patrolling nearby eyed them suspiciously. Naomi went straight for a small door in the side of the wall, where another Jewish guard stood post.

"The cook Naomi and her helper girl returning from the village," Naomi reported to the guard. He looked Tabitha up and down, trying to remember if he'd ever seen the child before. Then he stepped aside and nodded toward the entrance. Naomi pushed the door open and stepped inside. Tabitha followed, trying not to look at the guard. She closed the door behind them, and Naomi let out a sigh of relief.

"Safe thus far," she whispered. "But the real test will come later."

Tabitha decided not to ask what the real test would be, nor did she have time. She was instantly struck by all the noise and commotion. They had entered the kitchen of the palace, where servants were busy preparing the evening feast. No less than thirty women and men scurried about the room carrying platters and pots and piles of dishes. Steam rose from vats of boiling vegetables, smoke cuddled the searing chunks of deer meat over a fire, and round loaves of freshly baked bread filled baskets on a table in the middle of the room. Tabitha had never seen a place such as this, and she memorized every cook and candle and carrot to tell her mother someday.

Father! Tabitha thought, remembering why she was here in the first place. *I've got to find Father and return him to Mother!*

Naomi went to the fire pit and sliced off a chunk of deer meat. She tasted it, then sprinkled some seasonings over all the portions. "A bit more coriander," she said. "Coponius likes it that way." She told one of her assistants to let the meat roast a short time more, then introduced Tabitha to a boy of about twelve. "Simon, this is Tabitha," she said. "Instruct her well in how to serve the king." Then in a whisper she said to them both, "Her story is very much like your own."

"Yes, Naomi," the boy said, then turned and greeted Tabitha. "May you always find joy in your work here," he said with a bow.

"Thank you," Tabitha replied. "But I hope my work here only lasts this one night!" The boy looked shocked at this, so Tabitha gave him a quick explanation.

"Then may you have success in freeing your father," Simon said. "Now I must teach you what you must know!" With that, the boy began explaining the rules. "Always keep your head down and your eyes on the floor . . . You must take off your sandals before entering the throne room . . . Never turn your back on the king—walk backwards out of the room . . . Hold the serving dishes at arm's length in front of you . . ." And on and on until Tabitha thought they had more rules here than they did in Qumran.

Simon had just finished explaining the rules when Naomi announced it was time to serve. A dozen children lined up and each was given a dish to carry. Holding them out in front of them, with their heads down and sandals off, they all lined up, led by Simon. Tabitha stood at the end of the line, and then followed it down a hallway. Simon made a left turn through an arched doorway, and when Tabitha reached the same place she looked up and gasped.

Consider: What would happen if Tabitha let her fear rule her life, instead of trusting in God?

Part Two

On the other side was a room of marble large enough to hold her father's entire caravan with all its tents and animals. There were gold and marble statues all about, draperies hung between columns, and even a fountain on one side of the room. At the far end stood two thrones of solid marble, one larger and higher than the other.

The floor of the throne room was covered with colorful Persian rugs, and on top of these was a circle of men lounging on pillows. It was such a magnificent sight that Tabitha almost forgot to keep her eyes down, but remembered when she saw one of the men in the circle scowling at her. As Simon had instructed, Tabitha set her tray of meat in front of two men, then walked backwards out of the room. She couldn't help stealing a glance, though, at the two on the far side of the circle. One was a Jew, she could tell, sitting on pillows larger and higher than most. His face was sunken and his skin gray, but he wore a crown of gold on his head, and was covered with jewels and fine stitchery. *Herod!* she realized with a start. Next to him, on the highest and biggest pillows of all, sat a man in the uniform of a high Roman official. This must be the Roman investigator, Tabitha decided. *Copius . . . Corpulus . . . Coponius! That was it!*

By the time Tabitha remembered the name, she was out in the hallway. She stood and turned to follow the rest of the children back to the kitchen.

"She did well," Simon reported to Naomi, as the cook tested some quail meat.

"Then perhaps our plan will work," Naomi said, wiping quail grease from her lips.

"Nothing will work if my father's parchment does not arrive soon!" Tabitha cried.

Naomi thought a moment, then turned to the boy Simon. They huddled together, whispering for a moment, then Simon said, "Yes, Naomi!" and left through a side door.

"What is Simon doing?" Tabitha asked.

"A small errand," the cook answered. "Just in case . . ."

Naomi didn't say in case what, and Tabitha didn't have time to ask, because just then the head servant in the throne room rang for the next course to be served. Tabitha followed the other children once more—minus Simon—and then again some time later for the third and final course. Once back in the kitchen, Naomi wiped her hands on a cloth and said, "I fear the time of judgments has come."

Tabitha turned pale and her knees weakened. "Come," Naomi said. "We shall watch from the hallway."

Leading Tabitha back down the great halls, they peeked through the door the children had used to serve food. Tabitha saw that Herod was now seated on the lower of the two thrones at the far end of the room, and the Roman Coponius on the taller one. The other men who had shared the meal were standing along either side of the room, and were talking and laughing as if this were some great party.

"Bring in the first of the prisoners!" Herod roared, and a moment later Tabitha almost fainted as Roman soldiers pushed three men in irons through a side door.

The three men were haggard and bloody, having obviously been beaten by their guards. Tabitha watched as they were thrown down to the floor in front of Coponius, and was relieved to see that none of them were her father. A Roman soldier began reading charges against the men using words Tabitha had never heard before, words like *sedition*, *treason*, and *rebellion*.

A few moments later, Coponius raised his jeweled staff high over his head saying, "I pronounce the sentence of death by crucifixion!" He brought the staff down hard, the end of it making a loud *thud* on the marble. Instantly the three men were dragged away, and two more were brought in. King Herod, on his throne next to Coponius, sat giggling and clapping. *He sounds like a girl!* Tabitha thought.

In pairs and threes and some all by themselves, men—and even a few boys—were brought before Coponius for judgment. In almost all cases the sentence was death, except for the few boys who were sent off to work gold, copper, and salt mines for the rest of their lives. All of this took quite some time, and Tabitha's heart raced faster and faster with each new death sentence.

It stopped altogether when she saw her father brought in.

Eliakim looked much older than he had just a few days before, his face drawn and weary. So, too, did Hasbah and Uzziah. Irons connected by chains were on the wrists and ankles of the three, and they sounded a sad melody as the men trudged to a square of red marble in front of the thrones. Tabitha's Uncle Uzziah had bruises on his face.

Then Tabitha saw the Roman who had arrested her father, and she glared and gritted her teeth.

"I charge these men with treason, sedition, thievery, and making false claims of citizenship!" the centurion bellowed.

Coponius looked bored by now, as if he just wanted to get this over with. "Read the evidence," he droned. Even the men along the sides of the room seemed to be losing interest in the trials. At first they had cheered each time a man was sentenced to death. Now there was only polite applause.

"On a night six days hence," the centurion read, trying to make it sound dramatic, "your servant observed the prisoners attempting to make inconspicuous flight, hiding in their midst a girl disguised as a boy for some treasonous scheme against Rome. When confronted with their deception, the three attacked my squad, injuring three men with terrible bodily harm. Once subdued, the leader of the three made a claim of Roman citizenship, a claim he could not and has not verified to this day, and in fact has himself refuted by his own words and mannerisms, speaking often of the Jewish God as his Lord and Master."

Coponius was now mildly interested, and he stared at Eliakim. "Have you any words?" he asked.

Eliakim lifted his head, and Tabitha could see that it was painful for him to do so. "I have many words," he said. "Words of truth, words of honor, words of faith. But I have no words which you will believe, or which you will act on, even if you did believe."

Coponius stared again, surprised by the eloquence of the prisoner's speech. Wanting to be certain before pronouncing judgment, he asked Eliakim, "And what of this citizenship you claim? Why have you no proof?"

At that, Tabitha looked back down the hallway behind her, hoping to see Zechariah approaching. Of course, he was not.

"My citizenship is true," Eliakim said, his voice echoing off the walls of the great hall, "and I carry it with honor. It is a reward given me for service to Rome, and it is among my greatest possessions. My citizenship," he continued, "is as much a part of me as my heart, or my soul, or my Jewish heritage. It is with me in life, it will be with me in death. It is not something etched on a scrap of parchment."

"So you have no proof?" Coponius scoffed.

"The proof you seek I do indeed have," Eliakim answered wearily. "But in your haste for 'justice,' you will not be willing to wait for it."

Coponius eyed Eliakim for a long time. Then he sighed and said, "The law is clear and my duty written. I find you guilty of the charges, and I pronounce the sentence of death by crucifixion!" Coponius raised his staff high over his head, but before he brought it down and before she had even thought about it, Tabitha raced into the room and shouted, "Noooo!"

The Roman official held his staff in midair and stared at the intruder in shock. "Wait!" Tabitha cried, "I can prove he is innocent!"

Two guards grabbed Tabitha before she was halfway to the thrones. They stretched her arms out between them, and started dragging her back the way she had come.

"Hold!" Coponius shouted, and the guards stopped where they were. "Bring her forward," he said. "I will hear her plea."

All this time King Herod had sat on his own throne amused at the three shepherds before him. Now he laughed heartily at the spectacle of a girl trying to testify.

"Speak your words," Coponius said. "What is your proof?"

"My proof is in the very words of your own soldier," Tabitha shouted, pulling one arm free from her guard and pointing at the centurion who had read the charges.

Coponius's eyebrows shot up in surprise, and Herod giggled even louder. "Continue," the Roman said.

"Did he not say that these men disguised me as a boy and were smuggling me through the country for some evil deed against Rome?"

At this the centurion took a long look at Tabitha, finally recognizing her as the girl that had been with Eliakim.

"The girl he spoke of was you?" Coponius asked in surprise. At the same time Herod stopped laughing, and his eyes darted around the room, trying to figure out how the girl had sneaked into the palace.

"Yes, that was me," Tabitha said in a strong voice. "And that is the fact that proves he made up the whole story."

Coponius looked puzzled now, and shook his head slowly. "I do not understand," he said. "Explain yourself."

"Well," Tabitha said, trying to make her words sound as logical as those of her father, "if I am the girl they disguised as a boy, and if I was a terrible threat to Rome," she said, "then why did your soldier push me in the dirt and leave me behind? Why did he not arrest me with the others?"

Coponius stared at Tabitha for a long moment, then turned his gaze slowly toward the centurion. "Yes, that is an excellent question," he said. "Why is this so?" he asked the soldier.

The centurion turned pale and began to stutter. "I . . . I said that the men had *kidnapped* the girl—"

"That's not what you said!" Tabitha shouted. "You said, 'hiding in their midst a girl disguised as a boy for some treasonous scheme against Rome!'"

"She is correct," Coponius said. "I remember your words. So what is your defense?"

The centurion stood, silent, his face growing more red by the moment as anger and hatred and fear all fought for control of his thinking.

"I will deal with you in a moment, Centurion," Coponius said. Then he turned to Tabitha. "You have proven your point well," he said. Tabitha felt the tension flow from her body, and she felt herself breathe for what seemed like the first time in a week. "The charges of treason and sedition are dropped." A grin wider than the Jordan River crossed Tabitha's face, and she could almost feel her father's arms around her. But a moment later her joy turned to terror as Coponius said, "However, the charge of striking a Roman soldier still stands, and on that charge, I find you guilty."

"No!" Tabitha screamed, and once again the guards held her back.

Coponius raised his scepter high over his head. "I sentence you to death by crucifixion," he said.

But just before he brought the staff down with the thud of finality, a scream cut through the air that made everyone in the throne room stop and stare.

Consider: Tabitha was unable to change the sentence of death for her father. Sometimes we are unable to stop bad things from happening to the people we love. Does that mean that God isn't with us anymore, or that he doesn't care?

Part Three

Tabitha turned and struggled to see where the noise had come from.

"Tabitha!" a high-pitched voice screamed again. This time she found the source: her friend Simon, at a side entrance to the throne room. He had tried to sneak in but was caught by a guard, who now had the boy thrown over his shoulder like a sack of wheat and was taking him away. But then Tabitha saw something else: in Simon's hand was a scroll of parchment!

"Tabitha!" the boy yelled again, and Tabitha knew she had only moments to act. Her own guards had stopped to stare at the commotion and relaxed their grip ever so slightly. Taking advantage of this, Tabitha kicked her feet out from under her, dropping all her weight on her wrists. The Roman hands holding those wrists were sweaty with exertion, and Tabitha's fingers slipped easily through. In a second she had jumped to her feet and raced halfway to Simon.

Tabitha's guards reacted quickly, and were a few steps behind her. Simon was just being carried out the door when he gave the scroll a mighty throw. It landed on the shiny marble two steps in front of Tabitha, and she scooped it up without stopping. The guards dove at the girl and tackled her, but not before she had passed the scroll to her father as easily as when playing catch with her brothers. Eliakim caught the perfect throw with his chained hands.

Now Eliakim's guards grabbed for the parchment, but before anyone knew what was happening, he threw it at the face of Coponius, whose natural reaction was to grab the incoming projectile before it hit him in the nose.

The whole room froze in silence.

Roman guards stared at their leader, terrified of the wrath that was sure to kill everyone in sight.

Jewish servants stopped and stared, forgetting to keep their eyes to the floor, shocked as much by Tabitha's actions as by Eliakim's.

Eliakim and his brothers stared, wondering if their fate had just been sealed.

And Tabitha lay under two Roman guards and stared, wondering if she had been in time.

For a long moment, Coponius considered the scroll in his hand. *He must be deciding whether to read it or ignore it*, Tabitha thought. And she prayed to Jehovah that it was the former.

Finally Coponius lowered his arm. He eyed the scroll a moment longer, then, slowly, began unrolling it. He read it silently, then seemed to read it again. Finally he pulled it close to his face, staring at something in the bottom corner.

"Centurion!" he barked, and everyone in the room jumped at the sudden sound.

"My lord!" the centurion said, crossing his right arm on his chest and dropping to one knee.

"Why is it," Coponius continued, "that you have arrested a citizen of Rome without cause?"

The centurion looked up at his master in shock. "I . . . I had no proof!"

"Well, you have it now!" Coponius roared. "Release this man immediately, for he is not only a citizen of Rome, but a personal friend of Caesar!"

A gasp swept across the entire room, and people instantly started gossiping. "Do you see this seal?" Coponius continued, shouting at the soldier who even then was unlocking the shackles on Eliakim's wrists. "This is the personal seal of Caesar Augustus. You have not only shamed Rome by your actions, you have humiliated your Emperor!"

By now the three prisoners had been freed and the centurion was groveling at the feet of Coponius. Sensing that the tides had turned, the guards holding Tabitha let her free, and in two moments and three steps she was leaping into her father's arms.

"Father! Father!" she cried. She buried her head in her father's shoulder and sobbed in happiness and relief.

"There now, quiet, my little one," Eliakim whispered. "Jehovah has seen fit to keep me alive another day."

Coponius ordered the centurion arrested and taken from his sight. All of this amused Herod to great ends, and he sat on his smaller throne laughing merrily as the Roman was dragged out screaming.

"A fine show you put on, Coponius," Herod said between laughs. "First you free a Jew who strikes one of your soldiers, then you arrest your soldier for arresting the Jew, all at the bidding of a girl! Will you next make slaves of all the Romans to us Jews?"

Herod let out another hysterical laugh, but was cut off instantly when Coponius slammed his staff into the floor and yelled, "Silence!"

The room froze once again.

"You are mocking a citizen of Rome!" Coponius roared. "And because he is a citizen," he said, pointing at Eliakim but speaking to Herod, "he far outranks you, a simple Jew! And not only him, but his brothers, and his sons, and his wives, and even," he said with a glance at Tabitha, "his daughters! Take care what you say, 'king,' or I shall place this shepherd on your throne!"

Herod's face went stark white, then instantly flushed bright red. He struggled to his feet, facing Coponius, and Tabitha could see that he was weak and sickly. Six guards surrounded Coponius, their spears pointed toward Herod. "Take care with your words, Roman," he yelled. "I am Herod the Great! Friend of Caesar!"

Coponius shook his head slowly. "You may have once been great," he said, "but now your mind has gone mad. Do you not think Caesar knows about you? How you first plotted against him, and only joined his side when you saw that Antonio would be defeated? He called you friend because it was to his advantage. But now you have become a liability. Why do you think I am here, Oh Great Herod? Caesar himself sent me to investigate you!" Coponius leaned toward Herod and whispered loudly, "And if you do not soon die of your own diseases, I will recommend to Caesar that he order your death himself."

Herod was shaking, and Tabitha couldn't tell if it was from his fevers, fears, or anger. But a moment later he turned his back to Coponius and, with the help of his attendants, hobbled from the room.

With Herod gone, the guards stepped back, and the whole room relaxed. Coponius turned his attention back to Eliakim and said, "Now, my brother, would you care to tell me how you happen to know our Emperor?"

Consider: The letter from Caesar came between Eliakim and his judge to plead Eliakim's case. Hebrews tells us that Jesus stepped in to plead our case before God, saving us from death. What would happen if Eliakim, and you, both rejected such help?

Part Four

Eliakim bowed before Coponius, then stood and told his story. "It happened four years ago," he began, "in the desert of the Negev. We were camped some distance from Gerar, near the road to Beer-lahai-roi. I was riding my camel at sunset, scouting between the dunes, when I saw a small caravan in the distance. I rode toward them, thinking they perhaps needed my help." Eliakim took a deep breath, then continued. "The caravan was a small band of Romans—a few soldiers, a few advisors and priests, and a man who seemed to be the center of authority."

Pacing now, Eliakim rubbed his bearded chin, but was careful never to turn his back on Coponius. "As I approached, I asked if I could help," he continued. "One of the advisors mocked me, and said they needed no help from a . . . Jew. He started them off in a direction that I knew would lead them deep into the wilderness, so I followed at a distance. Soon a sandstorm hit, blinding the Romans and spooking their animals. When I heard the clamor, I rode ahead, and found the man of authority wandering on foot, far from the rest of the caravan."

Eliakim stopped his pacing and looked straight at Coponius. "He had been thrown from his horse, and was limping. I laid my camel down for shelter, and made a tent of blankets. I cared for his ankle and fed him well. We spent the night listening to the sand devils make their play. That's when he told me his name: Caesar Augustus."

A gasp crossed the room, and everyone stared in disbelief.

"We talked of many things throughout the night," Eliakim continued. "He was a curious man, interested in many things. Interested, especially, in King Herod."

Coponius's eyebrows shot up in curiosity. "And what did you tell him?" he asked.

Eliakim shrugged. "I told him the truth as I knew it," he said.

Coponius nodded. "And his reply?"

Tabitha thought her father seemed uncomfortable at the question, and she noticed he shifted his weight and looked to the floor. But she also saw a hint of a smile on his face.

"He said," Eliakim answered after a few moments, "that he would rather be one of Herod's pigs than one of his sons."

The whole room erupted in laughter, including Coponius. "And with that I would agree," he said. "Continue."

"In the morning," Eliakim concluded, "I gathered his advisors, who had scattered across the desert like seeds in the wind. Then I set them on a true course. But before they left, Augustus the Great made me a citizen of Rome, and wrote for me in his own hand the parchment you now hold in yours."

Coponius stared at the parchment reverently. *Augustus touched this very parchment!* his look seemed to say. Tabitha watched as he carefully re-rolled the document, then slid the binding ribbon back in place. "It is an honor to have in my presence one who both knows and saved my Emperor," he said, handing the parchment back to Eliakim. "Had we not just feasted, I would hold a great banquet in your honor."

Eliakim bowed again, and Coponius continued. "You shall have the protection of my best squad in all your travels," he declared, "and shall be given whatever provision you need. But first," Coponius said, "consent to stay with me a few days, that I may properly thank you for your service to Rome."

Eliakim bowed once more. This was a difficult situation, Tabitha could tell, because he could offend the Roman by refusing his invitation. *Be careful, Father,* she pleaded silently. *If you answer wrong, you may still die!*

Consider: Eliakim had compassion on his enemy even though he had no idea it would one day save his life. Do you think Jesus wants us to love other people only when it might someday work to our advantage?

Part Five

Coponius continued staring at Eliakim, waiting for his answer.

"I am but a simple shepherd," Eliakim began, "and not used to the rich foods and the rich ways of a palace. I have been gone from my family many days, and from my duties many more. With your permission, Oh wise ruler, I will decline your invitation, and go instead to find my caravan."

Coponius nodded his approval of this and said, "Foreign though our rich ways may be to you, it seems you have some rich ways of your own—rich in family and in honor. That I must respect. But do take my offer of protection, I beg. The forces of evil are strong these days. It is as if something terrible or something wonderful is about to happen."

"It is something wonderful," Eliakim said, "at least for my people. A new King is to be born, one who will teach us and guide us in a new way. Nor can I accept the protection of the Roman Legion: my God alone is my protector."

"Very well," Coponius said, "but I do not believe King Herod will much like hearing that another king is to be born."

"You are wise in this," Eliakim answered. "He will not be pleased at all."

"Answer me this, then, before you go," Coponius said. "Caesar Augustus is the ruler of Rome, and Rome is the conqueror of Palestine. When you found yourself alone with the leader of your enemies, hidden in a sandstorm in the middle of the Negev, why is it you did not simply kill him?"

Eliakim took a long moment to form his words as all eyes in the throne room watched. "The Romans are not our enemies," he said finally, and it caused a stir in the room. "Our enemy is our own selfishness, and sinfulness, and weak faith. But even if that were not so," he continued, "even if the Romans were our enemies, my God does not give me the choice to hate or not to hate, to kill or not to kill. Those decisions are for him alone, and my only choice is to love all people."

Now it was Coponius who took a long moment to think. Then he took in a deep breath and said, "Perhaps your God is more wise than I have believed." This caused another commotion in the room, but then the Roman ended the conversation by saying, "Go now, with the blessing of Coponius, the blessing of Rome, and in the guidance and protection of your God."

Eliakim gave one last bow, and was joined by Hasbah, Uzziah, and Tabitha. Then the four of them backed out of the room, and out of the sight of Coponius. Out in the hallway now, Tabitha jumped into her father's arms and hugged him as if she would never let him go.

"Oh, I have missed you so!" Eliakim said to his daughter. "I could not believe my eyes when I saw you in there!" He pulled her away enough to see her face, then asked, "How did you ever find me in this place?"

And so she told him. As they walked back to the kitchen, and met Naomi and Simon, and walked back down the hill where Zechariah was still waiting, she told them of all her adventures since their arrest. She told them of Decha in the desert, Qumran and Bartholomew, Seth and Zechariah, and Anna in Jerusalem. But when she got to the part where Simon threw her the scroll, she stopped with a puzzled look on her face. "If Zechariah is still down here waiting," she asked of Simon, "how is it you had the scroll?"

"This boy had the parchment for which I've been waiting?" Zechariah asked in amazement.

Simon hung his head shyly. "I . . . I know of a shortcut down the other side of the hill," he said softly. "I was afraid Zechariah's messenger would not return in time, so I intercepted him on the road, then ran the scroll up to the palace."

Everyone laughed and thanked the boy, then Zechariah said it was time for him to return to his home. Eliakim thanked the priest with a hug, saying he was sure he didn't know half of what Zechariah had done for his daughter. Then goodbyes were said with Naomi and Simon as well, and it was just then that a Roman soldier came down the hill leading Eliakim's three horses. They were loaded, Eliakim noticed, with food and provisions.

Anxious to be away from Herodium, Eliakim decided they would travel immediately to Bethlehem, where his caravan awaited. Tabitha thought that was a wonderful idea, and was still thinking so an hour later as they rode along in the moonlight. But a few minutes after that, she stopped thinking it, and let out a scream, when, amidst a cloud of dust and a flurry of hooves, they suddenly found themselves stopped in the middle of the road and surrounded by a circle of Jewish soldiers.

And there, in the lead chariot, sat King Herod himself.

Consider: Just when things seemed to be going well, Herod shows up. Just when our lives seem to be stable and happy, our own villains show up! Why doesn't having Jesus as a friend mean that nothing bad will ever happen to us again?

Part Six

Tabitha held tightly to her father's tunic. *No matter what*, she decided, *I am not leaving my father again*.

Herod stepped off his chariot and motioned for his men to pull Eliakim off his horse. They threw the shepherd to the ground, knocking Tabitha off in the process. True to her vow, she did not let go of her father, and landed on top of him in the dirt.

"So you think yourself better than a king," Herod said, looking down on Eliakim. "A lowly shepherd!"

Herod spat on Eliakim, but the shepherd said nothing.

"What's this? No clever words?" Herod taunted. "No great oratory about being a citizen of Rome?"

Again Eliakim remained silent.

"I AM HEROD THE GREAT!" the king roared. "I AM KING OF ALL JEWS! How *insolent* of you to think yourself better than me!"

Herod began stomping back and forth, pacing like a caged tiger. "Did *you* build the great fortress of Masada? Did *you* build the magnificent Caesarea? Or the palace of Herodium?" Herod stopped pacing and screamed in Eliakim's face, "DID YOU BUILD THE TEMPLE IN JERUSALEM?!"

The efforts of his rage caused Herod to double over in a fit of coughing. When he had finished, Tabitha thought he seemed near death. He looked out the corners of his eyes at Eliakim and said in a gurgled whisper, "I heard what you told Coponius. I heard about this new king to be born. Tell me now or die: Where is this to happen, and when?"

Eliakim pulled himself up straight and stared at the king, but said nothing. Herod nodded at his guards, one of whom stuck the tip of his spear to Eliakim's throat.

"Your Herodians may well kill me," Eliakim said, "but I will not reveal the secrets of the Messiah."

"Then kill you, they shall," Herod said, and nodded to his guard.

Tabitha screamed as the man pulled back his spear and re-aimed it at Eliakim's heart. But, just before his arm came forward with a fatal throw, the cry of "Attack!" came from somewhere in the surrounding hills. In moments the entire group was circled by a dozen Roman soldiers. The Herodian guards were swiftly disarmed and held by the Romans. As the dust of the scuffle settled, a Roman centurion walked calmly into the center of it.

The centurion stared at the king for a long moment, then said, "Leave, Herod. Or I shall finish the Emperor's work for him."

Herod scowled at the Roman, then abruptly turned and hobbled to his chariot. A moment later, all the Herodians were on their mounts and following their king up the road to Jerusalem. The centurion turned to Eliakim and said, "Coponius suspected your God might need a bit of help protecting you tonight."

"On the contrary," Eliakim smiled, "my God knew exactly what he was doing."

The centurion laughed, and offered to accompany the group to Bethlehem, but Eliakim assured him that all would be well now. And so it was, an hour later, that Tabitha, Eliakim, Hasbah, and Uzziah finally rode into the fields surrounding Bethlehem, and found there the caravan they had left so long before.

Consider: Sometimes it's scary to go before someone in authority—the school principal, our boss at work, a judge in a court. What do you suppose it's like to go before *God*?

Part Seven

Tabitha's mother screamed when she saw her husband, as did Hasbah's and Uzziah's wives. Tabitha hugged her mother and brothers, and stories of the day were told and retold around the campfire. A meal was prepared and bread baked. It is almost like a festival, Tabitha thought, only better.

Finally it was time to go to bed, and everyone said good night. Eliakim told his wife he wasn't ready to sleep, though, and would stand by the fire for a while. Tabitha couldn't sleep either, both from the excitement of the day and because her brothers were all snoring. So she lay on her bed, watching her father by the fire through the open flap in the tent.

And it was then that she saw a small boy pushing a cart across the field. She watched as her father talked to the boy, a boy who looked remarkably like . . .

Tabitha jumped up from her bed, pushed out through the tent, and ran barefoot across the field. "Jotham!" she called. "Jotham!"

The boy turned and looked. "Tabitha!" he yelled, then ran to greet her, and the two hugged in a great reunion. Tabitha's heart was so full of happiness she wasn't sure it could hold it all. But a moment later a thought struck her and she broke away from Jotham and ran back to her tent. Digging through a food bag, she found what she was looking for and ran back to her friend. She held out to Jotham a loaf of bread she had baked that very night and said, "I baked for you every day, just as I promised."

Jotham hung his head in embarrassment. "My mind would not forget you either."

Then Tabitha decided she should probably explain that there were a *few* days she had not been able to bake. She started telling him of all her adventures, about thieves and snakes and Qumran, about meeting friends and serving kings. But soon she could tell that Jotham wasn't paying attention. In fact, he was staring over her shoulder, looking at something behind her. Suddenly the boy walked right around her and off into the dark. "Jotham?" she said. "Jotham, where are you going?"

A moment later she understood. On the other side of the field was a shepherd at a fire, and Jotham was now running toward him, calling out, "Father! Father!"

And that's when Tabitha heard a woman scream.

It came from her right, at the top of the hill. A scream, she was sure. A woman. There it was again!

Without a second thought, Tabitha raced up the hill and into the town. She heard the scream again and looked around frantically. There, up on the left, she saw a glow of light coming from the stable below an inn. Another scream filled the air, and this time Tabitha knew where it came from. She hurried toward the stable, but before she got there a man came running up the ramp and ran right into her.

"Oh!" the man exclaimed, huffing and puffing. "Forgive me! But I need your help! Quickly child, run down to the next street, two doors on the right. Fetch me the midwife Dorcas!" The man's face was flushed and he seemed very nervous. "Tell her to come to the inn of Hasrah," he continued. "A baby is to be born at any moment!"

Tabitha almost laughed that the man was so afraid of a baby being born. But then she said, "As you bid!" and ran up the street. She found the midwife easily, then followed her back to the stable. There she saw the woman about to give birth, lying on a bed of hay next to a trough used to feed the animals. It was dark in the stable, with only the light of one small oil lamp pushing back the blackness. But even in the dim light, Tabitha could see the grimace of pain and the sweat of labor on the woman's face. It was a look she had seen many times before, when the women of her caravan gave birth. Still, Tabitha could see that the woman had a beauty about her that was more than just pretty eyes or a handsome face. She seemed to glow from within . . .

Tabitha gasped! This was the same woman she had helped on the road to Herodium.

"Do you think this will take long?" The voice startled Tabitha and she jumped. She spun to her right to see the husband of the woman wringing his hands and looking nervous.

"I do not know," Tabitha said. "Sometimes labor goes quickly, sometimes it's as slow as a donkey. Is this her first baby?"

The man got a funny look on his face, a look that seemed to have a whole story behind it, but he just said, "Yes, it is most assuredly her first child."

Tabitha shrugged. "Then it could take a very long time indeed," she said. "Only Jehovah knows."

The man almost laughed. "I will say amen to that!" he said.

Tabitha thought the man was acting strangely, but decided to say nothing more. She watched the woman in labor for a time, then decided she should get back to her own family. She turned and climbed the little ramp out of the stable, then made her way back to the fields of Bethlehem.

As Tabitha descended the hill, she saw Jotham in his father's arms. She met a woman confused by all the commotion, and learned that she was Jotham's mother. Tabitha led her over to be reunited with her son, then returned to her own camp, where she heard how Jotham had killed the old thief Decha.

There was great rejoicing among all the people then, rejoicing that Jotham had found his family, rejoicing that Decha of Megiddo was no longer a threat. Tabitha found her father amidst all the cheering and laughter, and gave him a hug around his waist. "I shall never again leave your side," she said.

She looked up into her father's smiling face and thought that nothing in the world could possibly be better than this.

In the next moment Tabitha was proven wrong as a bright light, brighter and more beautiful than any she had ever seen, filled the sky over their heads.

Consider: Imagine the most wondrous, glorious, fantastic thing that you could have or that could happen to you in the whole world. Now imagine something a thousand times better. That's Jesus! How should you respond to his love for you?

Christmas Morning

Light all of the candles.

Tabitha shielded her eyes and looked up. All around her women screamed and men drew their swords. The light spread out until it seemed to cover the entire sky, and everyone fell to the ground—everyone except Tabitha and Jotham. Then a voice, loud and deep, came booming from above.

"Do not be afraid," the voice said, "I bring you good news of great joy that will be for all the people." At these words the screaming in the valley died down. Some dared to take a peek through their fingers, and the men began to lower their swords. Every eye and ear watched and listened as they gazed at the glowing form above them, no longer needing to shield their eyes. The form was that of a dark-skinned man, with long, flowing hair. He was dressed in white robes with blue and purple sashes. He hovered in the air, light shining from his very being. He held a trumpet in his right hand and a golden scepter in his left.

"Today in the town of David," the angel continued, "a Savior has been born to you; he is Christ the Lord. This will be a sign to you: You will find a baby wrapped in cloths and lying in a manger."

Suddenly from nowhere there appeared thousands of angels, some near, some far. They covered the sky for as far as Tabitha could see, and lit up the world with their glow. And every single one of them seemed to be looking directly at her!

As they appeared, the angels began to sing. "Glory to God," they sang, and it was the most beautiful sound Tabitha had ever heard. "Glory to God in the highest, and on earth peace to men on whom his favor rests!"

Over and over the angels sang, "Glory to God in the highest." So holy was the sight that Tabitha might have been afraid, except that she saw her friend Jotham standing there, arms outstretched and eyes closed, turning his face to the sky as if to catch the light of the sun.

And then, quite suddenly, it was quiet.

People began to stand, and then they began to talk. In whispers, at first, whispers that asked, "Did you see that?" and "What could that have been?" Some were already saying it was a trick or a hallucination, but Tabitha knew better.

A moment later the realization struck her. "I was there!" Tabitha shouted.

Her father spun around from where he'd been talking with another man. "You were *where*?" he asked.

"I was right there in the stable," she said. "'You will find a baby wrapped in cloths and lying in a manger,'" she quoted the angel. "That's what he said, and *I was there!* At the stable!"

Eliakim was completely confused. Tabitha pulled on his hand and said, "Come on!"

"Come where?" the shepherd asked, even while obeying. "Tabitha, what is going on?"

Tabitha's mother hurried up beside her husband and talked to him as if he were the only one who didn't understand, which he was. "She was in the place where the babe was born!" she explained to her husband.

"Baby? What baby?"

Tabitha just shook her head and wondered why boys were so dumb, but didn't say anything. She led her parents and all their family up the path into town, and saw that Jotham and his family were ahead of them, with Jotham in the lead. Maybe not *all* boys are dumb, Tabitha decided. Somehow, she could see, Jotham knew exactly where to go, and led his parents down the little dirt ramp into the stable below the inn.

Tabitha followed a moment later, and saw that the woman had given birth to a boy, just as the angel had said.

Jotham was holding the baby now, showing the child to his parents. There was a commotion behind them, and then, through the door, Tabitha saw a face she did not expect to see. *Bartholomew!* Her friend from Qumran was followed by a man and woman, and Tabitha realized he must have found his parents.

How wonderful! Tabitha thought. *This child must truly be the Messiah, if his very birth brings together three children separated from their families.*

By now Bartholomew was holding the baby and introducing the child to his own parents, explaining that he, Jotham, and Jesus were all from the line of David. Then Bartholomew looked up and saw her. "Tabitha!" he cried, and everyone looked. Jotham and Bartholomew walked up to their friend and many introductions were made. Then Bartholomew asked, "Would you like to hold the baby?"

Tabitha's heart soared at the thought, and she almost said, "Of course I want to hold him. I'm a girl, and I can do it better than you!"

But then she stopped herself, lowered her head, and said to Bartholomew and Jotham, "You and Jotham should hold him. Both of you are his family, and I am but a simple shepherd girl."

Jotham and Bartholomew looked at each other and laughed. "What are you talking about?" Jotham said to Tabitha. "Girls are just as good as boys!"

"Yes!" Bartholomew agreed. "Have you not proven that many times? Now here, take him!"

And with that, Bartholomew placed the newborn babe in Tabitha's arms.

Tabitha pulled the infant up close to her face. She smelled his newborn smell, and touched the soft skin of his arms. The baby's eyes opened just a crack, and Tabitha felt as if he were looking right at her. She smiled, and whispered in his ear, "I will follow you always!"

Then she turned toward her parents, and with her brothers and uncles and aunts looking on she said, "Father, Mother, I would like you to meet Jesus, the Messiah, the Son of God!"

Glory to God in the Highest!
And Peace on earth.
For unto you is born this day,
and every day that you believe,
a Savior,
who is Christ the Lord.

Advent Through the Years

The following chart gives the Sunday on which Advent begins and the day of the week on which Christmas Eve falls, for the next several decades:

Year	Advent begins	Christmas Eve is	Year	Advent begins	Christmas Eve is	Year	Advent begins	Christmas Eve is
2010	November 28	Friday	2034	December 3	Sunday	2058	December 1	Tuesday
2011	November 27	Saturday	2035	December 2	Monday	2059	November 30	Wednesday
2012	December 2	Monday	2036	November 30	Wednesday	2060	November 28	Friday
2013	December 1	Tuesday	2037	November 29	Thursday	2061	November 27	Saturday
2014	November 30	Wednesday	2038	November 28	Friday	2062	December 3	Sunday
2015	November 29	Thursday	2039	November 27	Saturday	2063	December 2	Monday
2016	November 27	Saturday	2040	December 2	Monday	2064	November 30	Wednesday
2017	December 3	Sunday	2041	December 1	Tuesday	2065	November 29	Thursday
2018	December 2	Monday	2042	November 30	Wednesday	2066	November 28	Friday
2019	December 1	Tuesday	2043	November 29	Thursday	2067	November 27	Saturday
2020	November 29	Thursday	2044	November 27	Saturday	2068	December 2	Monday
2021	November 28	Friday	2045	December 3	Sunday	2069	December 1	Tuesday
2022	November 27	Saturday	2046	December 2	Monday	2070	November 30	Wednesday
2023	December 3	Sunday	2047	December 1	Tuesday	2071	November 29	Thursday
2024	December 1	Tuesday	2048	November 29	Thursday	2072	November 27	Saturday
2025	November 30	Wednesday	2049	November 28	Friday	2073	December 3	Sunday
2026	November 29	Thursday	2050	November 27	Saturday	2074	December 2	Monday
2027	November 28	Friday	2051	December 3	Sunday	2075	December 1	Tuesday
2028	December 3	Sunday	2052	December 1	Tuesday	2076	November 29	Thursday
2029	December 2	Monday	2053	November 30	Wednesday	2077	November 28	Friday
2030	December 1	Tuesday	2054	November 29	Thursday	2078	November 27	Saturday
2031	November 30	Wednesday	2055	November 28	Friday	2079	December 3	Sunday
2032	November 28	Friday	2056	December 3	Sunday	2080	December 1	Tuesday
2033	November 27	Saturday	2057	December 2	Monday	2081	November 30	Wednesday

Enjoy family stories by Arnold Ytreeide

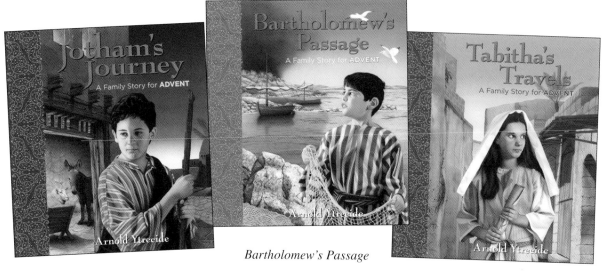

Jotham's Journey

Bartholomew's Passage

Tabitha's Travels

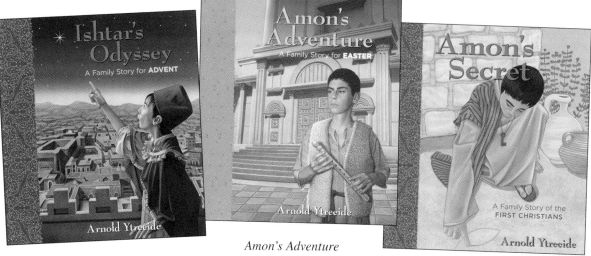

Ishtar's Odyssey

Amon's Adventure

Amon's Secret